THE REBEL AND THE ROGUE

INTERSTELLAR BRIDES® PROGRAM: BOOK 19

GRACE GOODWIN

GET A FREE BOOK!

INTERSTELLAR BRIDES® PROGRAM

YOUR mate is out there. Take the test today and discover your perfect match. Are you ready for a sexy alien mate (or two)?

VOLUNTEER NOW!

interstellarbridesprogram.com

1

Ivy Birkeland, Transport Station Zenith, Canteen

LEANING BACK in the chair I had tucked into the corner of the dark room, I scanned the area for threats. I ignored the large males minding their own business at the bar, although one in particular caught my attention. I wasn't here for *that* kind of meeting, but he was a sexy mountain of muscle and I was a red-blooded woman who knew what she liked. The hottie was Atlan sized, he made my usual issue of being too big obsolete.

The supersized aliens didn't mind my six-foot frame. In fact I'd had my share of offers over my four years in the Coalition Fleet. The job, though, had always come first. Discharged from service, I now had a different reason for being out here in space. A personal mission to bring a Cerberus asshole by the name of Gerian Eozara to justice.

A quest for justice that I could not walk away from or

deny, not without dishonoring my dead friends, dishonoring their sacrifice. Their memory. Their service.

Tears threatened and I blinked them away with a fury I rarely allowed myself to feel. Cerberus Legion was responsible for the Quell being sold in my sector of space. Quell was the reason I'd ended up crawling through the mud on Xerima, my friends dead, my body broken. When the Coalition Fleet's Intelligence Core had announced the bounty to catch the one who was responsible, I'd jumped at the chance to bring Gerian in, dead or alive. But a quick death wasn't enough for the Quell dealer and his cohorts. Torture would be better for him... and any other Cerberus scum I ran into.

Forcing myself to forget the past for a few moments, I enjoyed the vision of the big guy's tight ass and massive shoulders—I might be focused on my mission, but I was female. And his armband was green. Astra green.

This is not the alien you are looking for.

The mental play on *Star Wars* dialogue made me grin. Back under control, I looked around again. It grew later, the canteen slowly filling up with people in search of food or drink, of a semblance of normalcy in a place where nothing and no one was normal, at least not to me. More than a dozen conversations rolled through my mind in half as many languages.

Prillon.

Atlan.

English...

Turning my head to the right, I saw a handful of fresh, young, human recruits slamming shots of S-Gen whiskey like they'd just seen their first contaminated Hive soldier. Judging by the way their hands shook and the brittle natures of their false smiles, they'd probably just realized exactly what would happen to them if they were captured by the enemy. I'd slammed down half a bottle of space-made tequila after my first mission. My captain at the time, a no-nonsense military man from Italy, had let us all drown our sorrows in drink, carry each other off to bed and sleep it off.

The next day we'd all pretended nothing had happened, but the truth had been obvious. Scary as hell. No one in my ReCon unit—in all of the Coalition—wanted to be caught by the Hive. We'd rather die.

Careful what you wished for, Ivy. My mother's superstitious warnings echoed through my memories, and I rubbed the thick scar that ran from the base of my skull, down the back of my neck. Lower. Careful indeed. There had been many nights the last six months I would have rather been dead. Like the rest of my friends in my unit. Dead. Gone. Oblivious.

I grimaced at the bleak thought and swirled the dark gold tequila around inside the glass with my free hand. A full bottle rested on the table in front of me, but I hadn't touched it. Not one sip. It was a prop only, used to blend in. I needed my wits about me. This wasn't the place to stand out. Here, being noticed was dangerous.

Not for the first time I wondered what I was doing out here on the fringe of Sector 437, at *this* transport station, where criminals, spies and species from every planet interacted under the strict rules of the Coalition's Intelligence Core.

The rules were simple. No fighting. No killing. No violence allowed within the walls of Transport Station Zenith. Those who disobeyed were executed without question—if they were caught. Their goods confiscated. Their ships, too. Breaking the rules was rare, and those who did so were usually desperate and very, very sneaky. Or they wanted to die.

Since the transport station was within Battleship Karter's sector, barely, it *was* under Coalition control, which made it just safe enough to conduct *business* and just wild enough to keep respectable people clear. Or around for a purpose, like mine.

I used to be one of those people. Respectable. Now I was what I'd once reviled. I wasn't Coalition any longer. Obviously I hadn't returned to Earth after my discharge. No fucking way. I was a rebel in space, a Han Solo of sorts. It was funny how the will to survive could change one's opinion on just about anything.

I owed it to my unit—my dead friends—to see this through. I'd survived when they hadn't. I would not stop now. I would meet with the Rogue 5 operative, make the trade and get what I wanted: onto his home planet where I could hunt down Gerian Eozara like the animal he was.

Transport Station Zenith was a little rough, but I knew it had nothing on the infamous moon base my contact hailed from.

The meet wasn't for several hours. I had time to admire the huge male at the bar once more. The dark green band circling his biceps had the Astra Legion's symbol emblazoned in the center. I'd studied up on Rogue 5, knew the history.

Hundreds of years ago a Coalition ship of a few hundred fighters crash landed on Hyperion, a planet in the outer reaches of the galaxy. It wasn't part of the Coalition; therefore it lacked all advanced technology. From what I understood, the native Hyperion population had been a few steps up from Neanderthals, unskilled and lacking any advancements the rest of the universe utilized.

For some reason I couldn't fathom, some of the survivors from that crashed Coalition ship—Atlan, Forsian, Everian and more—mated with the Hyperions. Their ship was eventually repaired, and the survivors and their descendants rose from the surface, at least far enough to make it to Hyperion's moon, Rogue 5. There, the Coalition crew, plus those Hyperion they mated, created a base to be their new home.

In the centuries since, they had survived by their wits, doing whatever was necessary to protect their home. They were little more than pirates and rarely allowed outsiders into their midst, but their Coalition and Hyperion ancestry remained. Because the survivors there isolated, almost all who lived on Rogue 5 now had Hyperion blood. But they were all mutts and Rogue 5 was the pound. Some were Hyperion and Atlan, Hyperion and Viken, Hyperion and Forsian, depending on who mated with whom in their ancestry.

To make it even more complicated, the moon base was broken into five legions. *Everyone* was part of one legion. At Transport Station Zenith—which was probably the only place they comingled with others—I'd come across dozens of members from all the legions, could tell them apart by their uniform colors, the insignia. Astra was one of the more respectable, as criminals went. Styx and Kronos as well. But the other two legions—Cerberus and Siren? They were ruthless. Assassins. Murderers. Thieves. They trafficked everything from weapons to slaves with no conscience or remorse. I had a feeling the operative I would meet later would be wearing one of their two colors.

The Astra Legion's male at the bar was a forbidden fruit that I suddenly wanted very much to taste. Maybe I'd been wrong in my thinking. Maybe I could be here for my meeting and a little fun, too. When I'd been in the Coalition Fleet, we'd been told to steer clear of anyone from Rogue 5, regardless of their legion. They *were* rogue, just like the name of their moon base. Wild. They'd be called bad boys on Earth. No way could they measure up to Coalition standards.

But when it came to sex? Screw rules and regulations. I had no doubt he'd be as wild as his home world. The bad boy from Rogue 5 would be really, really good. I had no doubt he'd be up for a good time. A quickie. It had been a while since I'd had a male-induced orgasm, and based on the size of him, I had to assume he was proportional. *Everywhere.* My pussy clenched at the thought.

As if he knew I was thinking about him—and what he could do if we found the nearest horizontal surface—he turned and met my gaze.

My breath got trapped in my throat, and a flush of heat went through me as if I'd downed a few shots of the tequila. Holy shit, he was hot.

I pegged him at six-nine, two seventy. Easily. He was the largest male I'd ever seen, and I'd fought alongside Atlans in beast mode. He put football players, human strongmen competitors, hell, even mythical Vikings to shame. He had black hair and eyes so dark I couldn't see the difference between iris and pupil. From across the room I couldn't miss the sharp cheekbones and square jaw. Regal nose. Full lips. If he had on glasses and a tie, I'd rip open his shirt and find a giant *S* emblem on the shiny suit hidden beneath. His superpower would be panty destroyer, because mine were ruined.

The latest version of a superhero movie had come out just before I'd left Earth and volunteered for the Coalition, and this guy was a darker alien doppelgänger of my favorite ass-kicking hero.

He was going to fuck me. I was confident about that. Besides womanly instinct, his gaze didn't falter, only raked over my face, my mouth, what he could see of me sitting down.

One look from him and lust burned through me until I trembled with it. I'd eyed a guy across a bar before, on Earth. Flirted. Fucked. I was a woman and I had needs, nothing I was ashamed of. But I was more aroused by just eyeing the alien before me than I had ever been from any guy on my home planet. Hell, any guy I'd *ever* slept with.

The alien was... potent, and that was at twenty paces. If he touched me...

I licked my lips, trying to imagine what he would taste like on my tongue, feel like beneath my hands. The small flicker of my tongue over my lips made his gaze narrow, and he moved toward me like I'd tied a rope around him and yanked on my end. Hard.

No one got in his way. No one dared.

He stopped on the opposite side of the table. Looked down. Pheromones pumped off him. He exuded sex, even *smelled* like it, and I had to plant the soles of my feet onto the floor in a conscious effort to keep myself from standing. Because if I stood, I'd move. And if I moved, I'd be wrapped around him in half a second flat. I'd climb him like a monkey, and that wasn't the way to go unnoticed around here.

"You shouldn't be here, female." The deep rumble of his voice rippled across my skin like the bass beat through a speaker, and my nipples were instantly hard as rocks.

As they said on Earth, those were fighting words. Now that I was out of the Coalition, no one told me what to do.

"I can take care of myself," I countered with a snap, eyeing him. Hell, eye *fucking* him. I took my time, inspecting every perfect inch. Those lips. So full. So firm. His disapproving gaze encouraged me to defy him all the more. I didn't see fangs, but then I'd heard they only came out when these Rogue 5 hybrids took a mate. Since I *definitely* wasn't his mate—I belonged to no one—it meant I wouldn't get that experience, which was just fine with me. I liked sex a little wild, but fangs and biting?

He studied me in silence, and I stared back, refusing to look away. The standoff made my pussy wet with heat.

"Hey, Lieutenant? You all right?" One of the humans from the ReCon unit nearby called out to me and I frowned. Damn it. I'd been honorably discharged from the Coalition Fleet, but my neural implants were still active and could be scanned by other fighters if they were wearing their Fleet uniforms loaded with active tech. That tech in the newest outfits constantly scanned for friend and enemy alike, picking up Hive frequencies no matter how subtle.

When Prime Nial of Prillon Prime, the leader of the entire Coalition of Planets and the big boss in charge of all the military, said veterans contaminated with Hive tech could go home, well, figuring out who was going to be dangerous and who wasn't had become a pretty big priority for the Coalition Intelligence Core. No one wanted a warrior, fighter or warlord with implants to get pinged with Hive signals and go on a killing spree.

So the new uniforms had scanners, and all service members had transmitters imbedded in their flesh that those uniform scanners could read. Bad news for me at the moment. Once a lieutenant out here, always a lieutenant, even if I didn't wear the uniform.

Before I could respond, the giant alien in front of me

growled, the sound a low warning to anyone who might think of interfering.

The ReCon team stood as one, their hands on their blasters, ready to take on an alien from Rogue 5 for me, which meant they would die.

Brave but stupid. No doubt the whiskey had clouded their heads beyond safe levels.

I rose and put my back to the alien, a calculated risk that made my skin tingle and my entire body want to weep with pleasure. Maybe he'd wrap a hand around my neck and pull me to him. Perhaps he would spread my legs and take me from behind while everyone watched. Somewhere in the last few years my fantasies had grown dark and needy. Taboo on Earth. Too wild.

Shoving those thoughts aside, I held my palms out toward the table of honorable fighters who were just trying to protect one of their own. It wasn't their fault. "Stand down, ReCon. I'm fine. Don't break the I.C.'s station rules for me."

The man who'd spoken tilted his head and, looking over my shoulder, sized up the Rogue 5 male. "You sure, Lieutenant?"

I didn't bother telling him not to call me that. He wouldn't listen. "I'm sure. Thank you. Enjoy your time off." I thumbed over my shoulder and grinned like I was sharing a secret. "He's a friend."

That brought a round of chuckles from the group and one wide-eyed look full of envy from the single female among them. "Damn. You go, girl." She grinned back and raised her glass in salute just as a very large hand came to rest on the curve of my hip. *His* hand. His warm, heavy, even bigger than I'd imagined hand. God, yes.

I grinned back at her, wrapped my hand around as

much of the large male wrist behind me as I could, and blindly dragged the alien male toward the nearest door.

Shoving it open, I pulled him through—I was well aware he was allowing me to do so—and slammed it closed behind me and activated the lock. Fortunately, we were in a deserted gaming room filled with more than a dozen empty tables, chairs and the space version of billiards.

When I turned around again, it was to find him grinning down at me, his cock an obvious and very large bulge beneath his uniform. I'd been right, he *was* proportional.

"Are you sure you don't want me to be on Zenith Station? It'll be really, really hard"—I glanced down at the *hard* cock I wanted him to think about—"for you to fuck me if I leave. And it will be impossible for you to do so with your pants on." I pressed my back against the door to bar any kind of escape.

One dark brow winged up, but he said nothing. He wasn't leaving. Oh, he was big enough to pick me up and handily move me out of the way, but he wouldn't. Not with his cock pressing thick and long beneath the black fabric, and getting bigger as I watched. How had he walked around the canteen with that? How was it not busting out the seams?

I licked my lips, realizing all of that was for me. *Because* of me.

My eager need wasn't as readily apparent, but if he were an Everian Hunter who could scent a female's arousal, he'd know my pussy was hot, wet and primed for him. He could no doubt see how hard my nipples were. Space bras weren't anything like the Victoria's Secret bits of lace and satin I used to wear on Earth. But after four years with the Coalition Fleet and the last six months as a bounty hunter roaming the rogue-controlled fringe areas of space, I'd learned a space guy—an alien—didn't give a shit about lingerie. Or weight. Or height. Bra size. High heels. Makeup. Hairstyle or what name-brand handbag a woman carried. None of the things I'd grown up worrying about.

Coalition or not, these alien males liked a female *willing*. Bare. Wet. Ready. And if she wasn't any of those things and he wanted her, he'd get her that way.

This male would find out soon enough I didn't need any help in that department. Except maybe for the naked part. I was already wet, willing and ready.

I wasn't worried about foreplay, and I didn't want to know his name. Neither were needed. Hell, just looking at the gorgeous specimen of a stranger was all the warm-up necessary. Because, wow. I wanted hot, wild sex and no strings. I wanted him. Now.

"And it will be impossible for me to lick that pussy with you wearing yours." The deep rumble that was his voice had felt like a challenge out in the canteen. His current words were one sentence of foreplay. But the promise I saw in his gaze and the thought of what he planned to do to me caused a whimper to slip from my lips.

He heard it, and the corner of his mouth tipped up.

Damn and holy hell, he was too gorgeous to be real. But he was here, living, breathing, eye fucking.

Real or not, I wanted him to lick my pussy. God, yes. I was horny. I wasn't ashamed. I was single. Alone in space. I wanted some cock, and I was going to get it. The dinner I'd eaten earlier had filled my body. I'd craved the food, and it left me sated. Now I craved *him*, and I wanted *him* to fill my body. He'd leave me sated, too, but in a completely different way.

"You're still dressed," I said.

His gaze darkened, his voice dropping to a growl.

Another challenge that made my legs tremble. "So are you."

For two people who wanted sex, we weren't getting very far. We were at a clothing stalemate. We were positioning, testing our power, who would dominate. At this point it was even.

I liked that. A lot. But I knew he was holding back, could turn me and take me against the door at any moment. Knew that I wanted him to take me, make me wild, give me no choice but to let go and give in to the pleasure.

But I would never admit that, not to a dominant, bossy male alien like him. Because if I did, he'd want to own me. So I would give him the green light, get his cock inside me, and hope like hell he was as wild as he looked.

Our hands went to our clothes at the same time. It was as if we'd both reached the tipping point of need and neither of us wanted to pretend for another moment

Shutting out the world, my mission, my past, everything but this moment, this little sliver of time, I focused on him until he was all I saw. All I wanted. And we *still* hadn't gotten to the good stuff.

My shirt went flying. His boot bounced off the wall where he kicked it. Pants dropped. We were both bare within seconds, everything we wore like a yard sale around us. There was only a locked door between us and the full canteen. The knowledge of that, the rush that someone might discover us, made this all the hotter.

The air was cool on my heated skin. When his gaze raked down my body, taking in every inch, I shivered. I wasn't perfect. I had every feminine doubt Earth's culture bred into women. I wasn't a supermodel, not before the accident and definitely not after. I had a scar running down my neck and half my spine. A big scar, one giant among dozens of smaller battle wounds I'd earned the hard way. A

ReGen pod could heal a lot, but not if it took too long to get in one. Not after the body had begun to heal itself. Even after ten hours in a pod, my scars remained, and I waited for him to notice the marks visible on my thighs, abdomen and shoulders, waited for some kind of reaction.

He stared at me all right, but his gaze flickered past my scars like they weren't there. Instead he focused on all the *right* parts and in a *very* appreciative way. For him I was tall enough, but my boobs were too big, my hips wide. My ass... well, my ass was glorious. It was my vanity.

The way he licked his lips, it seemed he liked a whole lot more of me than my ass.

And him? Holy fuck. He was like Michelangelo's David combined with huge alien hunk. Slabs of muscle. Shoulders as wide as Texas. Narrowed waist. Slim hips. That V thingy that made my mouth water. And between that V... porn stars would bow down to this cock.

It wasn't so huge the size scared me, because who wanted to be fucked with a lead pipe? But it was big. Stretch me open and maybe hurt just a little, big. My pussy clenched in anticipation of this masterpiece before me. Thick enough he would open me up, rub over every hot spot I had and probably discover some I never knew were in there. Long, but not so long as to break me. I'd take him all, barely.

I liked the idea. A lot.

"I want you inside me now," I said.

He shook his head as he slowly approached, his cock bobbing hard and erect before him. It aimed, pointed at me as if it knew I was its next conquest.

"No."

No? Fuck, yes. I shivered. His denial made a bolt of electricity run through my flesh.

2

He was naked, stalking me, and he said no?

"Now, female, I lick that pussy until you scream."

Oh. I retreated, leaned back against the door once again. With that one step, triumph flared in his eyes. He'd declared the dominance here. But when he dropped to his knees and pushed my legs wide with his hands on the insides of my thighs, I didn't care.

"You are scarred," he commented as his palms felt the blemished flesh. His gaze raked over the pink and white tracks, remnants of my personal nightmares.

"So?" I asked defensively. Good thing he hadn't seen my back. If he didn't like what he saw, then he could just fuck himself.

"So where I come from, they are a sign of bravery. Of life experienced. Of honor."

He looked up at me from his position on his knees.

I had no idea what to say to that, for it was completely not what I was expecting. I didn't want to *like* this guy; I just wanted to fuck him.

"You talk too much. Less talk, more licking," I ordered.

No woman breathing would say no to this guy eating her out. I might be brazen, but I wasn't stupid. And I wasn't into self-denial, either.

I wanted those lips on me. I wanted that tongue. Those hands. The long fingers. I didn't want praise.

I shouted when he gave me all those things at once. A long slide of his tongue up my slit. Hands on my ass tugging me closer. Fingers tightening on my hips so I'd know I wasn't allowed to move, that he had no intention of letting me go until I came all over his face.

His mouth settled over my clit, sucked, his tongue working magic. My eyes fell closed, but he lifted his head to say, "So greedy."

My fingers tangled into his hair, tugged him back into me. I felt the smile against my lower lips, his satisfaction at my need clearly amusing him.

"I pulled you in here, didn't I?" I breathed, tilting my head back as he easily worked me. My orgasm swiftly approached; he was that talented. Or I was that horny. Or both.

He growled, turned his head and nipped the inside of my right thigh and I pressed hot, sticky palms to the door behind me, used it for leverage. "Your ability to talk indicates you are not satisfied with my attentions. I shall remedy that now."

"Oh fuck," I whimpered, then nothing else. It was as if he shifted and went into pussy-eating high gear.

I couldn't talk after that, only moan, beg, whimper. His mouth was on my clit, a finger inside my pussy and doing some magic curl over my G-spot. The thumb of the hand cupping my ass pressed against my back entrance, adding even more sensation I hadn't known existed.

"More," I said, and he pressed the thumb deeper until it breached me, until he was fingering both my holes. I'd never had anyone do that to me before, never knew I wanted it. Until now. I didn't have to be shy or vulnerable or hell, even think. If I wanted his thumb in my ass, then I was going to tell him to put it there.

I didn't have to worry about a thing with him because I didn't even know his *name.* This was anonymous. Hot. Crazy. Perfect.

Lifting my sweaty palms from where they were pressed into the door, I cupped my breasts, tugged on the nipples. I needed even more stimulation, and I added it. The combination of his mastery and my hands pushing myself to the brink made me gasp. Writhe. Something sharp nicked my skin, just a bit. Quick, like a jolt of static electricity going straight to my clit.

I came on a scream, my knees buckling, my hands slapping against the door as if it would hold me up.

I heard the clatter of things striking the floor just before my back hit a flat surface. I hadn't noticed much of the room when we entered—I co uld hardly see around the huge alien—but I knew he had swept a gaming table clear, the items scattering and rolling on the floor as I tried to catch my breath.

He stalked toward me, his mouth glistening with my arousal. His eyes narrowed. His cheeks were flushed with desire. So was his cock. He wasn't Atlan but looked like one in this moment, as if he had a beast beneath the surface ready to break out and wreak havoc on my pussy.

This guy's beast was between his legs, and there was no question it would own my pussy.

"Your scream of pleasure pleases me," he said, wrapping his fingers around my thighs and slowly pulling me toward the edge of the table. "No doubt everyone in the canteen knows how well I've satisfied you."

God, that should have mortified me, that I'd given over to him so much I'd forgotten where I was. I should have been embarrassed or ashamed that everyone in the canteen would know exactly how he had wrung the scream from me, that he was proud to share his virility with the entire space station. Instead the naughty factor made me hot. If he could do that to me with just his mouth, then I was going to love what he did with his cock.

The table was made for us, high enough to get my body's needy core close to him. To his cock. It was at the right height for him to only need to bend his knees a little to be aligned.

"The way your body clenched and tightened. The gush of your nectar." He licked his lips.

"Are you a poet?" I asked, coming up on my elbow, reaching out and gripping his cock—as best I could—in my hand. I gave it a tug, a long stroke. Felt how smooth the skin was, how hard beneath. How long. Thick. Pulsing with heat.

He hissed.

"I am male, satisfied by my female's response to my touch."

I stiffened at that. "I am not *your* female. This is one time only."

He grinned then, feral and broad.

"Um... what are those?" I asked, my gaze focused on the

sharp tips of his canines. Holy shit, he was part Forsian. A Rogue 5 guy with Forsian ancestry. Just as I'd learned about Forsians—I'd done a lot of studying up about the planets once I left the Coalition—he had vampire teeth, but now they were on display and the idea of being bitten by him wasn't nearly as abhorrent as I'd hoped.

"Fangs."

I shook my head. "Don't you dare bite me. I want hot sex, but biting? Not a chance. I don't want a mate."

He gently tucked a strand of my hair behind my ear, which contradicted every wild thing we'd done so far. "I will not bite you. As you said, we are together for pleasure. Nothing more. These"—he slid his tongue back and forth over the sharp tips—"are for claiming a mate."

I licked my lips. pushed up to sitting, and he stood between my spread knees. He wasn't getting inside me until I knew the score. On Earth it would be about safe sex, about using a condom, protection. Birth control. That had been taken care of for me by the Coalition. Kids weren't happening until I was ready.

But biting? This was the weirdest conversation ever.

"Do not worry, female. To claim a mate, I must bite and fuck at the same time."

His cock stood long and thick, ready.

"Same difference," I countered. "The plan was to get that big dick in me, but how do I know you won't bite me?"

He shrugged slightly. "I slid my fangs along your inner thigh."

"Holy shit, you bit me?" I put my hand over the spot, remembering the exquisite feel.

"No. You will know when I bite you."

"You won't be biting me," I countered.

He tipped his head. "You *would* know if I bit you. But I

won't. You have my word. I promise you. I *vow* not to bite you."

"Then why did you *nip* my leg?"

He smiled, those fangs long and lethal looking. "Because I wanted to."

Oh God. That was hot. Too hot. His chest was hard and huge and right in front of me. His cock was hot and ready, and my legs were spread open around his hips. All I had to do was take him. "But—"

"I will get my cock in you as you desire," he said, speaking over me. "It's going to happen, human, but even if you begged, you would not get my fangs. It would be too dangerous." His hand moved down the center of my body to my core, his fingers sliding over my sensitive folds, entering me easily because of how wet I was.

My back arched. He was playing me. Working my body to make my mind forget.

It was working.

"I will not lose control. You trust me with your orgasms. Trust me in this."

It was the way he touched me, almost reverently, which was completely at odds to how we'd been behaving, that had me nodding. I didn't know him, but I did trust him in this. Why? I had no fucking idea, but it seemed he wanted a wild fuck for a short time, not a mate for life.

"We've spoken too much," he said, pulling his hand from me, lifting his fingers and licking them clean.

I whimpered again at the loss of his touch, at how blatant he was in his sexuality, in wringing the same from me.

He stepped even closer so his cock was pressed against my belly. "There is only so much time before I must leave you. Do you wish to talk or take my cock?"

I laid back down, set one foot on the table so my toes curled over the edge, then the other.

He growled at the sight of me open and ready for him.

He could lean over and bite me, but like this he could fuck and keep his distance. The last thing I wanted was to be mated to a strange alien with fangs, no matter how glorious his dick. And I knew he spoke the truth. He was a hybrid Forsian, like Makarios of Kronos. The item I'd brought in trade to my Rogue 5 contact would help him later, once I was gone. I liked the idea of that. And the truth was, I wasn't afraid of his bite. It wouldn't kill me like he presumed. I wasn't exactly a *normal* human female. But I didn't want a mate, that was for damned sure.

I had things to do, people to meet, problems to solve.

I didn't need a Superman in my life, and I knew enough about the Forsian hybrids—Forsian mixed with Hyperion that populated Rogue 5—to know that one bite of those fangs and he'd be thinking I belonged to him forever.

No, thank you. I was not the settle-down kind of woman. Not yet, anyway. I had a mission, a very dangerous, very personal mission to complete before I could even think about anything permanent. Vengeance. Revenge. Redemption. I had stopped asking myself why I needed to finish this and accepted that I wouldn't be able to stop until the criminal who had killed my entire ReCon unit was dead.

Dead or alive. I preferred dead, but the bounty set out by the Coalition's Intelligence Core wasn't specific like that. Dead or alive was the official line. But that decision was for later. I'd meet my contact from Rogue 5, trade what I had for a ride into their fortress of a moon base, capture Gerian Eozara and end this.

That didn't mean I couldn't have some fun in the

meantime. And this massive male was exactly what my inner sex-starved goddess wanted. Big. Hard. Willing.

And no strings. For once Fate seemed to be on my side.

His hand went to the base of his cock, worked it so the tip slid up and down my slit. I gasped, lifted my hips for more.

"Like this?" he asked, his gaze meeting mine.

"Put your cock in me, Forsian. Now," I growled.

He grinned ferally and plunged deep.

My back bowed, my body rippled and stretched to take him.

"Fuck," I moaned.

He pulled out slowly, slammed deep. "Yes, female, now we fuck."

His thrusts were so powerful his hands went to my hips to keep me from sliding across the counter. He'd been gentle there for a moment or two, but that was no longer.

He was intense, forceful, his gaze on me, watching my breasts sway, my mouth open on a gasp. The way sweat broke out on my skin. The way I gripped the edge of the table with my fingers as if I needed to hold on or fly away.

"Yes," I begged.

His pace was deliberate, focused, as if every time his cock filled me it was intentional, the motion, the speed, the angle were all deliberate. He grabbed an ankle and wrapped my leg around his hip. I took the hint and hooked both behind his back. I wouldn't have been able to do it if I didn't have long legs. He was so big.

Now we were joined, locked together by me, his motions minimized by the hold. A hand hooked behind my back and lifted me up so I was impaled on his cock. He pivoted, pressed me into the wall.

There was nowhere to go, no give. Nothing to do but take

the pummeling he was giving me. He hit deep, stroking over spots I didn't even know I had.

My breath came out in pants, and with each one I took in his scent. Sweat, virile male and wild sex. His skin was hot, slick with sweat.

Because of his height, his back was curved, his mouth by my ear.

"You want it."

"Yes," I replied, my eyes falling closed.

"Take it."

"I am," I growled.

"Human, look at me."

I did, got lost in the fathomless blackness of his gaze. The way his jaw clenched, the fangs peeking out from between his lips. The bead of perspiration slipping down his forehead. The feel of his hands cupping my ass. The thrust... fuck, the deep penetration of his cock. He was in me. Surrounding me. Looming. Taking.

"You will come when I say."

I shook my head, my hair sliding along the wall. "You don't control me," I panted.

He smiled wickedly, leaned in, slid his teeth down the length of my neck. I felt the sharp tips, knew he just had to press and he'd bite. But he didn't.

I shivered.

"Don't I? Why haven't you come then?"

I pushed at his chest, but he was like the wall behind me, unmovable. "Listen, you Neanderthal—"

"You are impaled on my cock. You can't go anywhere. My fangs are an inch from your neck. Your pussy is milking me, eager for me to empty my balls. You came on my mouth, you will come on my cock. Not because you will it, but because I command you."

"Command me?" I snarled, tried to lift off him, which only made his cock move inside of me even more. "We're fucking. Why are we arguing?"

"Because you won't submit."

I bared my teeth now, all but growled at him. "Never."

It was a silly vow, for he was right. He was bigger than me, stronger. I was caught on his cock. I couldn't get off this ride unless he allowed it.

"If you didn't want this, you wouldn't be dripping all over my balls. You like what I'm doing."

"Like you said before, if I'm talking, then you're not doing it right."

His brow winged up.

He unwrapped my legs, bent his knees so my feet touched the ground and pulled out. Before I could ask him what the hell he was doing, he spun me about, gripped my waist and lifted me up onto the counter so I leaned over it. The cold surface made me gasp. My legs dangled down, and because of the height my feet didn't touch the ground. One hand was on my upper back, holding me down.

Again I waited for some sign of rejection from him. He had full view of my scars now. I tensed, expecting him to ask questions I didn't want to answer. Or worse, walk away.

"Human, you have experienced much," he murmured, his palm sliding down my spine, down the length of my scar. "So brave, so strong. Fuck, I shall cum just looking at the mark."

I had no idea what that meant. What guy blew his load for a hideous marring of skin?

Instead a thick thigh nudged mine apart as a big hand came down on my ass. The slap stung but didn't hurt. "You doubt me," he commented.

I shook my head. I didn't want to talk about the damned scar. "Fuck me."

He spanked me once more but didn't lift his palm again, only gripped the right cheek and pulled it open.

"Pussy or ass, human?"

I looked over my shoulder at him. He was not even looking at my scars. His gaze held mine, lust and need there that he didn't even try to hide from me. God, he was so hot. His body was all taut lines, his cock dark with blood and glistening from being inside me.

He waited, which was ridiculous because he had to be hurting with need to be back inside.

"Pussy," I breathed, realizing he wouldn't do anything until I answered. I'd never done ass play before, and I wasn't going to start in this moment, not with the huge cock and without any lube. Besides, he was bossy already, I didn't need to surrender more to him.

Fuck, he was dominant. And in this position—

"Oh my God," I breathed when he slid inside me in one slow, deep thrust.

One hand hooked my shoulder, the other remained on my ass as he took me. I couldn't do anything except take it.

He leaned down, and I felt his tense muscles, the heat of him.

"You will come when I say and not before."

I gritted my teeth, wanting to tell him off, but I couldn't. I liked this. Loved it. I didn't have to think, to worry, to wonder if he liked my body. If he found my skill as a lover to be too much or not enough. If I was making too much noise, not enough. If I was too forward. Bold. If I was too marred to be beautiful. All I had to do was take everything he would give me, and I would like it. No, I'd love it.

His thumb found my back entrance again. Circled, teased. I clenched down.

"My balls are eager to empty. You will come with me."

I shook my head, stared blankly out into the empty room, but I wasn't disagreeing. I was... giving in.

One thrust, then another and I was done for. So was he.

His growl ripped through the air, cut the silence like I knew his fangs would cut me. But he didn't. While he controlled me, he controlled himself, too. I could let go, give in to every base instinct I had, but he couldn't.

It was that one thought that pushed me over—besides the huge cock, the thumb pressing my ass open, the feel of him behind me—and I screamed again, this time silently.

I was lost. Wild. The orgasm was so intense, so powerful no sound came, only feeling. I bucked beneath him, completely out of control. His large hand held me down, pressed me flat to the table as he pumped into me, fucked me through my release, prolonged it with every hard stroke into my sensitive, swollen pussy. He moved until I couldn't.

I slumped onto the table, done.

I heard his ragged breathing, felt him pull out, lift me so I stood up, albeit on shaky legs.

We didn't say anything as we dressed. I was sore, achy. I felt used in the best of ways. My muscles were lax, my brain mush. He'd done *everything* I'd wanted in a quick fuck, and then some. I had to wonder if I were ruined for anyone else.

I cleared my throat, thinking of that tequila. I could use a shot. Or five.

"Thanks," I said. After what had just happened, I didn't have to worry too much about making small talk. We weren't dating. I wasn't his mate, and he wasn't mine. Fact was, I'd probably never see him again.

He looked at me as he buttoned up his pants. It was a shame to put such an incredible cock away.

I turned, unlocked the door, left. It was over. Fifteen, twenty minutes of the wildest sex of my life. But that was all it was. A quickie in an empty room. Orgasms shared. World rocked.

Mission accomplished. It was now time to move on to the next one, to find the Rogue 5 operative and make a deal.

3

enos, Astra Legion, Transport Station Zenith

THE DOOR SILENTLY SLID OPEN, and I stepped inside one of the most opulent suites on the space station. Before me sat Astra, our leader, surrounded by several other members of the legion. She never admitted her age, but we all assumed it was somewhere in the middle of her fourth decade. Her long hair was pulled back in a tight braid. The strands were streaked with gray and every bit of clothing she wore was Astra Legion's dark green. She looked relaxed in pants, a tunic and soft-soled boots, but I knew that was a facade. Somewhere, hidden within the folds of her clothing, would be both a blaster and several blades.

Astra had not held power over the legion for more than twenty years by taking unnecessary risks. I'd seen her kill with an efficiency many envied, but always for her people, for the legion. That's why we were loyal to her. She'd earned the right to lead us, her devotion and protection as fierce as any male's could be. Perhaps more so because she was female, a matriarch, the ultimate protector. She never placed her own needs above the needs of her people. Never.

Much to Barek's disappointment. He wanted Astra for a mate. The other hybrid Forsian males knew this fact to be true. Astra, however, seemed oblivious to his interest, even as he sat beside her now. Or perhaps she pretended ignorance to avoid the inevitable confrontation of what could never happen.

In the end they could never be together, not if one bite from his fangs would kill her.

I entered and took a knee a few paces from where she sat, head bowed, waiting for the questions and the permission I needed to fully enter her domain without the giant hybrid Forsian male at her side ripping my head from my body. They were not mated, but Barek protected her as only a true mate would, without mercy or divided loyalties. He didn't leave her side. Not to eat. Not to sleep. Not to fuck. He slept on a thin mat outside her door, guarding her even as they slumbered. He was hers.

The others sat around Astra at a small table. They were gambling. Drinking. Killing time and keeping their minds off the mission ahead of us. I'd gone to the canteen for a drink, to sense the mood of the transport station. To listen to what was going on around us. Astra had sent me because out of all of us, I was the most subtle of the bunch, which was truly absurd. The group from Astra Legion were all here for one reason and one reason only, to obtain the antidote to a hybrid Forsian's bite.

I was *far* from subtle, and the hot human whose taste was still on my tongue knew that well enough.

"Where the fuck have you been?" Barek asked.

I did not envy him his devotion to this female. His

mating instinct, nearly as strong as the Atlan's fever, had been riding him hard the last few months. If he buried his cock in any willing female in his current state, he'd probably kill her. If not with the poison in his bite, with the sheer strength in his frame. Since his cock wanted Astra, he wouldn't kill *any* female, he'd kill the leader of the Astra Legion.

Some of us born on Rogue 5 had inherited a deadly cocktail of Hyperion heritage mixed with Forsian DNA. As a result we endured both a blessing and curse. We were bigger and stronger than any others on the moon base, larger even than the few Atlan hybrids. But it turned out the Forsian part of our physiology did not blend well with a Hyperion male's mating venom. A pure Hyperion male on the planet below Rogue 5 would bite his female to induce a state of arousal and fertility, to increase her pleasure. But when mixed with Forsian bloodlines, that venom became a deadly poison.

We few hybrid Forsians who survived on Rogue 5 were doubly cursed with the locking mechanism of the Forsian mating cock and the Hyperion instinctive need to bite our females. The two instincts were so deeply ingrained in our natures that most females on Rogue 5 were not willing to take the risk of bedding us at all, not even for one night of pleasure. When we found a female brave enough—or adventurous enough—to express interest, we always ended things after one or two sessions of sex. We never kept any female close for an extended period of time. Hybrid Forsians always distanced ourselves before the instinct to permanently claim the female we fucked overwhelmed our self-control.

To die with honor was preferable to killing a female during a failed mating. In all my life, I'd never heard of one of us successfully claiming a female until Makarios of the Kronos Legion. I'd heard horror stories from the past, stories of females dying in agony as the males who loved them looked on in helpless agony and guilt at what they'd done.

Bitten her. Injected her with poison. Lost control.

More than one female had accidentally been killed by her lover over the years. Those of us with honor did not take a female to bed unless we knew we could control the urge to bite. To mate. To claim.

And that was one of the reasons the hybrid Forsians on Rogue 5 were dying out, born from those bite-free one-night stands. Without a true father. Without mated parents. Most Forsian hybrids refused to lay with a female, afraid to lose control. But now, Makarios of Kronos had become a legend among us. He'd disappeared, then turned up alive on The Colony, his body enhanced with Hive technology. That was fact, what we knew to be true. After that, we knew nothing. Had the Hive integrations been what had changed him, had the Hive made it so that Makarios no longer had the poison in his fangs? Or, as rumor claimed, had his female, a *human* female, actually created an antidote to the poison? Had she found a serum to counteract the venom in my fangs? In Barek's fangs? In the fangs of all the desperate hybrid Forsians left?

We were here to find out. Anxiously awaiting the upcoming meeting. To finally get our hands on this *supposed* antidote.

Fucking a stranger made denying the basic instinct easier, but still difficult. And the female I could still smell? Still taste?

Gods help me, I'd never had my fangs descend during sex before.

I wanted her. Badly. And more than once. My cock was still hard and eager for her. Her denial, her refusal to give me her name, had only made me crave her more. I felt wilder than usual. Hyperion DNA made all of us wilder, difficult to control. We had fangs, each and every one of us. We bit. We fought. We raged. And our new people did not fit into the Coalition worlds. *Especially* the few of us who had poisonous venom in addition to our ion pistols and lethal blades.

I was a hybrid freak who would never set foot on the planet Forsia. I was blessed and cursed. Barek and I, and the other hybrid Forsians like us, were not built to mate. Yet we craved what all males did: hot, wet pussy. Soft cries of pleasure from a willing female. Release.

Peace.

I'd found it for the short time with the human. Despite my eager cock, my balls were drained, my body relaxed for the first time in forever. She'd been insatiable. Passionate. Powerful in the knowledge of what she wanted. Shared it with me, with words, with her body. She wasn't an Everian virgin. She wasn't what I'd expected from a human, for they were small and weak.

Not her.

No. She'd taken everything I gave her, and I hadn't gone easy. It wasn't in my nature. I fucked wild. I fucked hard. I fucked to ensure she'd feel me for days.

And she'd not just cried out with pleasure, she'd demanded more. Needed everything I had to give her.

With my return to the suite, the sated pleasure I'd enjoyed bled away. Reality returned, and I found Astra watching me with raised brows, realizing I'd never answered Barek's heated question. "Well? Where have you been, Zenos? I sent you to the bar two hours ago."

"Drinking." My answer was one word, but I knew it would be enough. No one would assume I had been with a female. Not me. Not a hybrid Hyperion animal who'd gotten the worst of two worlds, a cock that swelled and locked our female in place, a mating instinct so strong it could drive us mad, and poison in our Hyperion fangs deadly enough to kill with one bite.

"Do not lie to me." Astra spoke, her voice stern even as she ignored me now to stare at the small, square cards in her hand. "You smell like sex."

"Yes. A distraction to help pass the time." No sense denying it. Rumor was, Astra had Everian Hunter's blood in her veins. The gods knew she could smell better than any living being should wish to. I didn't like having poisonous fangs, but I'd hate to be able to pick up scents as acutely as she did. And smelling sex on another? No, thank you.

"Did you kill her?"

Practical. That was our Astra. Our leader. I did not know her true name, the name she's been given by her mother. When one assumed head of a Rogue 5 legion, the leader embodied all that we were, including the name. That day, when I was but a small boy, she had become simply Astra. She led us, not like the Coalition where there was a chain of command, but as a large family. A brotherhood of sorts, led by a matriarch. We lived by a code, her code, an ethical standard—which some might consider hypocritical. Whether or not the Coalition of Planets considered something illegal was of no concern to us. What the other legions did was of no concern to us. We did what was best for our legion, for our people, for our common good. We didn't fight the Hive. We fought the other legions of Rogue 5. For territory, for survival. Astra Legion didn't peddle slaves. Didn't sell Quell. Didn't think second and kill first like Cerberus or Siren Legions. Astra was too smart for that.

But that didn't mean we weren't ruthless. As leader, Astra was the most lethal. Cunning. Brutal. She was feared by the other legions, and rightly so.

"She lives," I replied. "I did not harm her." She might have bruises upon her soft skin from a tight grip as I fucked her, but nothing that would not fade, nothing she would not look upon and remember how I'd made her scream. There was no doubt she'd feel me for days. My cum was probably dripping from her well-fucked pussy at this moment.

The female fascinated me, and I knew I would think of her often. Wonder how she'd obtained the magnificent scar that ran the length of her back. She'd been bothered by it, not proud. A human instinct perhaps to see the scar as an imperfection, not *perfection*. The thickness and size of the mark had made me fuck her harder. Faster. Deeper. That mark of strength and courage, of survival, had made my instincts roar to claim her. To bite her. To keep her.

"Tempting the gods is not wise, Zenos." Barek chastised me, but I did not respond. I knew the battle he fought every day with Astra so close to him. The words were for himself, a reminder, as much as for me.

Astra grunted and laid down her cards, which caused the others to grumble and hand over their credits. Three hybrid Forsians were in this room, and there were less than twenty of us anywhere in the galaxy, all of us sworn to Astra Legion. Except Makarios from Kronos Legion. Outsiders believed there were only three or four hybrid Forsians under Astra's control, and our leader liked it that way.

Makarios had broken from the fold years ago and served Kronos Legion. But he'd been older than the rest of us. When he'd sworn allegiance to Kronos, he'd been just a boy and the leader of Astra had been a brutal ass. But then Makarios had been captured by the Hive and assumed lost. Wrong again. He'd shown up at The Colony, enhanced with cyborg parts. He'd been strong before. I couldn't even imagine what the Hive had created. He must have hated every moment of it, surrounded by Coalition fighters, the only one from Rogue 5.

And now? He was truly a legend. Mated to a human female who had killed a Nexus Unit and stolen a ship. Makarios was gone from Rogue 5, gone from every space station from here to Xerima. The Coalition was hunting him. We were hunting him. The other legions were hunting him. I'd heard that even the Hive were hunting him... or his female.

We'd all heard odd stories of his human female being one of *them,* that she could transform into one of the blue creatures that led the Hive, the Nexus Units. I had no idea if that were true, and Astra didn't give a shit if she was blue, purple or human, she wanted the antidote Makarios's mate had supposedly created. She was truly mated to him. Had survived his bite. We all needed mates to help us survive. To keep Astra legion strong. Astra wanted that antidote for her hybrids. We weren't going to lose our minds, as the Atlans did in their Mating Fever, but without mates, we suffered as they did. We hybrids just lived with the pain in our bodies.

It would almost be a relief to be Atlan, to know there was an end to the hunger and madness. To know that without a mate to keep us sane, we would be put down. But we were not so lucky as the Atlans. And I had no desire to die.

I wanted that antidote. We all did. If I'd had it, I wouldn't have ridden the edge of insanity as my cock filled and fucked that lush human. Her skin had been sweet on my tongue. So had her pussy. I'd grazed her tender skin with my fangs, the need within me insisting I plunge them as deeply as I had my cock. I'd been desperate to make her writhe and moan for a completely different reason. I had almost lost control.

Almost.

I'd held off, barely. Kept sane. Barely. I liked her alive, panting and moaning, whimpering and screaming because of me. Because of pleasure. Not pain.

Had I been able, I would have filled her with my cum for hours because of the mating fist, marked her over and over with my bite. Made her mine—no matter that I'd told her otherwise—and dealt with her anger about it later. But that wasn't an option for me. For any of us.

We were strong. Mean. Bigger than any of the other races and fiercely loyal. If Astra—the female, not the legion —lost us, her power position on Rogue 5 would be dangerously threatened. The members of the legion would be threatened. No doubt Cerberus or Siren would attack while the legion was weak. Take Astra Legion's women and children, sell our people for slaves or mercenaries.

Astra appeared to be satisfied with my response. "Anything out of the ordinary? Anything to report?"

"Nothing. Everything appears to be normal. I do not believe we are walking into a trap."

She tipped her head toward one of the bedrooms. "Get cleaned up. We leave soon."

I grunted and moved to do as she ordered. I washed in a shower tube and hated that I rinsed the female's scent from my body. Her taste from my mouth. Her soft whimpers from my mind.

No, those I'd never forget.

When I emerged a short time later, I was in full legion armor. Stolen from the Coalition—we'd taken their latest technology and adapted it to our needs. Instead of gray and black, we'd altered the color to black and dark green and emblazoned Astra Legion's emblem on both shoulder and chest. Our dark green armbands, worn at home over more traditional and casual clothing, were part of the uniform rather than an adornment. The suit would deflect small blaster fire and protect us in the event we needed to evacuate or enter the cold dark of deep space.

With every layer of protection I added to my body, I drifted farther away from the female and focused on the mission. We would meet with the Coalition fighter who claimed to have the antidote, Astra would bargain and we would leave. There was no other alternative, not if I and my fellow hybrid Forsians wanted to mate, wanted to have children. Peace. A reason to keep going.

Astra had changed as well, her soft, flowing tunic and pants replaced with her own, much smaller battle armor. We didn't know what we'd be facing, and we didn't know who to trust. To outsiders we seemed wild and disorganized, but we were far from it. There was no dissension in the ranks; there were no ranks among those of us in this room. We all served Astra and we needed the antidote, so everyone worked together for it. A common goal, a common purpose.

Astra looked me over, the lines around her eyes and mouth making her look fierce. "We are not coming back to this room. We don't dare. Nevuh and Rhord have gone ahead to ready the ship. You and Barek will accompany me to this meeting. We leave with the antidote at any cost. Do you understand?"

Barek and I both answered. "Yes, Astra."

We would acquire the prize at any cost, even it if meant taking what we wanted and leaving the Coalition contact dead.

Barek took his usual position ahead of Astra, and I fell in behind. It would take a small army to get through us, and even if someone made it to our leader, she was deadly in her own right.

We arrived in the empty meeting room well ahead of our contact, exactly as we had planned. I took my place hidden in the shadows as Astra sat at the single long table. Barek stood behind her with his arms crossed. We were heavily armed, the blasters at our sides misleading. It was the blades tucked into our armor that we preferred to use to make an honorable kill.

Long minutes passed as we waited in silence. When the door to the room finally slid open, I kept my gaze on Astra. She would signal if she wished me to appear. Until then, I was to remain hidden. She didn't want to frighten the Coalition contact. Astra wanted the antidote, and she preferred not to kill. Not here. Even Astra would not be immune to the Intelligence Core's justice should we break their rules for the space station. If we killed, we would have to fight our way back to our ship.

I watched as Barek stepped forward. "Sit."

His order was clear.

"I think I'll stand, big guy. Thanks anyway."

The voice that replied made my chest tighten with pain. My cock instantly surged to life, hard as stone.

"Sit!" Barek bellowed, but I already knew how this was going to go. I knew exactly who had entered the room. I knew her voice. Her breathy cries of pleasure. Her scream of release. And I knew, even before Barek's fists tightened at his sides, that this particular human female was going to defy him.

4

"THAT WILL DO, BAREK." Astra put out a hand and waved him behind her. He complied, but not without glaring at the human female whose sweet scent I had just washed from my cock.

Astra took her time studying the lieutenant, the Coalition female I'd fucked hard enough I had to wonder how she could walk so steadily. No question her pussy was sore. I imagined that if I tugged down those pants, I'd find her wet, swollen and coated in my cum.

"I offered you a seat out of consideration, my dear, but you may stand if you choose." Astra's voice was smooth. Even congenial. It was all a lie.

"I do. Thank you." And I knew the female's words were also false. She wasn't thankful. She was appeasing, for now. Falsehoods on both sides.

Astra drummed her fingertips on top of the table, and

my body tensed with every small beat. "Have you brought what you promised, fighter?"

"I'm not a Coalition fighter," she snapped.

"That is a lie," Astra countered, her voice slightly raised as she pointed to a readout on her modified Coalition armor. "You are a ReCon lieutenant, of Earth."

My female—fuck—the *Coalition lieutenant* dealing with Astra shook her head. "Not anymore. I ran ReCon for four years. Now I'm... retired."

Damn it all, not knowing her name while we'd fucked had been sexy. Hot. Her insistence on anonymity had made my balls tighten. Now I wanted to know my opponent, to have the edge on her. I wanted to know everything.

What retired *human* Coalition fighter spent her time negotiating with someone from Rogue 5? Spent her days at a transport station in the outer reaches of Sector 437 where nothing good ever happened to beautiful, small females without a mate to protect them?

Her.

My cock punched against my armor, eager to get inside her again. She was fierce. Brave. Crazy. And I wanted her again. I felt my fangs elongate, but I willed them back.

"I see." Astra raised her brows, and I couldn't stop myself from sliding to the side, just far enough to peek around the large pillar hiding my body from the lieutenant's view. The darkness would be enough to conceal me, I was sure of that. And if it didn't? I didn't really give a fuck, not with the way Barek was opening and closing his fists as if he wanted to *punch my female.*

What if I was wrong? What if his fangs had elongated as well as his cock?

Mine.

The thought burst to life inside me, and I didn't fight it

this time. I wanted this fearless human female again. And again, I wanted to fuck her until I forgot to breathe...

"If you are retired, what are you doing here?" Astra asked. "Why did you not return to your home world?"

"Earth?" She laughed. "As if. There is a bounty on Rogue 5 I wish to collect. My price for the antidote is safe passage to your moon base and shelter within Astra Legion while I hunt. That is all."

That was all?

Did she understand the risk to Astra Legion if our leader granted her request? Anyone this female hunted would also be seen as a target of Astra. If this female took shelter in our legion, wore our colors, Astra would be held accountable for anyone she hurt, anyone she killed.

And what was this small, weak female thinking, trying to hunt on Rogue 5?

Her bold declaration made my balls ache to fill her again. A bounty hunter? She was a fucking bounty hunter? And she wanted to get *onto* Rogue 5? Had she lost her fucking mind? The first words I'd said to her in the canteen were that she didn't belong out here, in this area of space. She was human. Small. Weak. If she didn't belong on Transport Station Zenith, there was no fucking way she would survive on Rogue 5. She'd be dead in a matter of hours.

Apparently, Astra was no more convinced than I. "All you want for the antidote is passage to Rogue 5 and a safe place to sleep?"

She nodded. "Yes."

"And this bounty you are hunting? Is it one of mine?"

"No, Astra. I would not insult you in that manner. The criminal I hunt runs with the Cerberus Legion. He's a Quell dealer. He sold a bad mix to my ReCon unit. Got them all killed."

I wrapped my fist around the blaster at my side and grimaced as it crumpled like paper under my grip. Cerberus? If they caught my lieutenant, they'd do worse than kill her. Far, far worse.

No. No. No. No...

"What is his name?" Astra asked.

"Gerian Eozara."

I'd never heard the name, but that was no surprise. I preferred to stay away from all members of Cerberus Legion, from any legion other than Astra, for that matter. No recognition flickered on Astra's face; therefore she was either extremely good at hiding it or she didn't know him either. It didn't matter, the name—they were all lawless fuckers in Cerberus.

"I know of him," Astra said. "He is well known for cutting his product with other, less expensive, materials."

"Less expensive? Is that what you call sending an entire ReCon unit on a bad trip?"

"I do not understand this term. Where did they take this trip?"

The human sighed, hands on her hips. "Hallucinations. Made them see things that weren't real. Bad things. By the time the Hive showed up, they didn't know what was real and what was the drug. Got them all killed. Every single member of my unit died that day."

"Yet you survived." There was a question behind Astra's words.

"I did." The two words held finality and didn't invite more questions.

Guess Astra wasn't going to get any more information from the female, information that I desperately wanted.

How had she received the scars that covered her body? Had it been during this battle? How many times had she fought the Hive? ReCon units were known to infiltrate Hive infested areas and attempt rescue operations. Very dangerous work. The idea of my female...

No. Not mine. Never mine.

"I am sorry for your loss."

"Sorry isn't enough for me. I want Gerian's head on a spike."

That made my leader smile. "Understandable. I accept your offer." Astra's words made my body heavy as lead, but I should have known the worst was yet to come. "Assuming you have proof that what you trade is the true antidote to hybrid Forsian poison. How do I know what you offer is, indeed, the formula that made Makarios of Kronos Legion able to take a mate?"

The lieutenant crossed her arms over her chest. I knew what those lush curves looked like bare. Had watched as the soft, pink tips hardened. "I took the antidote weeks ago, when I tracked my bounty to Rogue 5."

"Did you?" Astra's voice sounded... intrigued. "And what proof do I have of your claim?"

My female shrugged as if Astra's question meant nothing. She pointed to Barek. "Have the big guy here bite me. He's part Forsian, I assume. If I'm lying, I'm dead."

What the fuck?

Astra's entire body went still, and blood pounded through my head as I waited for her response. She was my leader. I was blood sworn to follow her orders. But this? No. Gods help me, no.

Bite her? Barek?

No, Astra. No.

"If you are lying, you will die," Astra warned.

"I know. Do it. Tell him to bite me." The defiant human raised her hand, one finger pointed up in the air and her brow arched high above one eye. "But no mating bullshit. This means nothing, big guy. We clear on that? You try to mate with me, and I will kill you."

The human female had fallen directly into Astra's hands. If she lied, she'd die. Astra didn't have to raise an ion pistol to kill her for playing us. The human would kill herself, and we wouldn't have to worry about Coalition rules.

The lieutenant hadn't blinked an eye. In fact she had suggested it. Was she so daring she was willing to risk her own life, or was she telling the truth? Bluff or bravery?

At the slight nod from Astra, Barek moved forward toward the female. *My* female. "My bite will make you scream, female. Then we will see if it is in pleasure or in death."

"Just shut up and do it." The lieutenant tugged the armor away from her neck, exposing the long, bare flesh I'd recently kissed. Sucked. Tasted.

My mouth watered as she angled her head to the side.

Barek got closer. He looked at Astra, something dark and dangerous in his eyes. Was that need? Regret? The room was too dark, but Astra seemed to sense that he needed something from her. "Nothing will change, Barek. Bite her."

Barek nodded slightly and turned his attention to the human. Moved.

Closer.

He leaned over her and opened his mouth. I saw his fangs. Her smooth, pale skin. So soft. So sweet. So damn mine. He didn't want to do it. I knew it. The only female he wanted to sink his fangs into was Astra. But it was her order, her command, and he did her bidding.

The lieutenant stood as still as a statue, her gaze locked with Astra's in stubborn defiance.

Fuuuuuck.

My body moved before I could regain control, the bellow from my lungs one I'd never heard before. I was on him before anyone in the room could react. I picked up my longtime friend and threw him across the small room, where his body smashed several inches deep into the wall. He slid to the ground with a grunt but was on his feet in seconds, fists clenched, death in his eyes.

Astra launched from her chair and stepped between us, and by the gods, that was the only thing that kept me from killing him.

"Enough." Astra waited for Barek to nod before turning to face me—and *her*. She looked us both over for long, silent moments. "This is the female you fucked."

She didn't question, she knew. Most likely scented me on the human And that made me growl, knowing the female walked around with my scent, my cum all over her.

"Yes." There was no use denying it.

I looked to the lieutenant. Her mouth hung open, eyes wide. Clearly she hadn't been expecting to see me ever again. She'd been cool and confident facing a leader of a Rogue 5 legion but was stunned dumb by the sight of me. I wasn't sure if I should preen or growl.

"Then you will do it," Astra said. "Bite her."

Behind me, the lieutenant gasped. "No. Absolutely not."

I looked down at her, the brave face she'd worn until now completely gone. She looked... shaken.

Oh shit, had she been bluffing? Was I the one to kill her then?

Astra was ruthless. "You will accept the bite of one of my Forsian hybrids, or the deal is off."

The lieutenant shook her head. "No. I have the antidote, I just don't want *him* to bite me."

Her words crushed something dark and hungry inside me. She had taunted Barek into biting her. And yet with me, she refused as if I were less. Not worthy.

She would not choose me. She would never choose me. But perhaps I could help Barek and the others. "We must not bite her, Astra. The risk is too great."

That made Astra's gaze snap to attention, her interest in my protest immediate.

"You refuse my command to bite her, Zenos?"

Her words were formal, and I knew I was on very dangerous ground. She'd probably known the second the female entered the room that I'd had her. The test, it seemed, was as much for me as for the lieutenant.

"Yes. The risk to"—fuck, I didn't even know her name —"the Coalition lieutenant is too great."

"I could have you executed for this," Astra warned.

I bowed slightly. "I accept your judgment, Astra. My loyalty to you is unchanged."

"What?" Behind me the female stepped to my side, her face lifted to study mine, but I held Astra's gaze. This was no small thing, but I would do anything to make sure Barek didn't touch her. That none of the other Forsians would touch her. I'd rather be dead than watch Barek taste what should be mine.

"What are you doing?" the lieutenant asked. "I'm telling you, it's fine. Let him bite me."

"No!" My response was immediate and far too loud.

"You don't have to protect me. You don't even know my name."

Turning from Astra, I looked down at the female. "Does it matter?"

"It does to me. Ivy. My name is Ivy Birkeland."

Nodding at the honor she'd given to me, I turned back to face my leader. "We will not risk her life, Astra. I cannot."

"I see." Astra studied us both as Barek paced behind her, waiting for her decision. His cock was hard, his fangs extended. He wanted to bite a female, but I wasn't sure whether it was Ivy or Astra driving his need.

Not Ivy. Never my Ivy. Over my dead body.

"Very well." Astra's words drained the tension from my muscles, and I noticed Barek relaxed as well. Fucking volatile bastard. But now, with Ivy standing next to me and the mating instinct riding me as never before, I began to understand his struggle with our leader.

Ivy jumped into the silence. "I have several doses of the antidote hidden in a lockbox with a transport beacon attached. Only I have the transport code. Once I am safely on Rogue 5, I will give you the coordinates and you can transport the antidote samples to your labs."

The breath left my lungs as Astra glared at the human female. She was either the bravest I'd ever met, or the most stupid human ever to transport off planet Earth—and my female was not stupid. Insane, but not stupid. She had the scars that proved it.

"If you fail to deliver the antidote, I will slit your throat myself."

Ivy nodded. "Fair enough. Let's go."

Astra shook her head. "Not so fast." She looked up at me. "Zenos, because you refuse to bite her, we do not know if she is lying or if the antidote she offers is effective. The only way to test the truth of her claims is for her to be bitten."

"I will not risk her life," I repeated. Not my lieutenant.

Better to test it first, allow our scientists to examine the formula. "Let the scientists decide."

"I have agreed to this against my better judgment, but she will be your responsibility, Zenos. You will ensure her safety until we have the transport code. After that, you will present her to the others on Rogue 5 as your mate, your female."

"What? Wait!" Ivy Birkeland countered.

Astra looked her dead in the eyes, her ultimatum quite clear. "You wish to remain within Astra Legion, to hunt someone from Cerberus? You will not travel alone, nor hunt alone. You are under my protection, and I am responsible for your actions while you are in our legion."

Ivy was silent, and Astra turned to me. "If her bounty, this Gerian Eozara, as she says, is a member of Cerberus Legion, you will assist her in bringing him to justice. I hate those scum. However, if she lied to us, you will bring her to me. And if she dies while under my protection, you had better be dead first. Do you understand?"

"Yes, Astra." I understood perfectly. Ivy was mine, but not the way my raging cock wished. No, I had to watch her, protect her, help her and keep her out of trouble until Astra had the antidote. Without biting her. After that? If Ivy told us the truth, she'd be fine. If not? Astra didn't make idle threats.

5

Ivy, Traveling to Astra Legion, Stealth Ship Legacy

WE'D BEEN STUCK in these cramped quarters for hours. Barek watched me like I was going to stab Astra in the back at the first possible opportunity, and Zenos looked at me like I'd already done so, but to him. It wasn't my fault they didn't believe me. Well, Astra might have believed me, but she saw it more as an opportunity for me to prove myself in the most lethal of ways. If I lied, I died. She couldn't have asked for a better situation.

That was fine with me. I'd taken the antidote. I knew I was safe from the poison. I just wasn't safe from a big hybrid Forsian who could do magic with his cock.

I'd learned that all four of the guards she'd brought with her to Transport Station Zenith were hybrid Forsians, and that these males along with a few others in the Astra Legion were the only known hybrids in existence besides Makarios. And since he was the one who'd successfully mated a human without killing her, these others were the only males in the universe who needed the antidote in order to claim a mate.

That meant finding a soul mate, a partner in life... a bride of sorts. Children. Love. A bonding. Things everyone deserved.

The fact that Astra was willing to risk taking me into her territory in order to acquire the serum for these males said a lot about how much she valued them. Rumors circled that there were more of them, but nothing I could confirm, and I didn't care enough to investigate. Astra cared about her people, and that care and concern included Zenos.

When I'd asked Astra about the rumors of even more hybrids, Astra had dodged the question, but Barek had scoffed at the idea and Rhord had glared. Just like Zenos was doing now. I wasn't in this for the friendships. I was in this ship for revenge. For Gerian Eozara. They didn't have to like me.

"There's no need to stare. I'm not going anywhere," I snapped, addressing the male whose cock I'd had inside me, the male who acted like I belonged to him now. Zenos of Astra Legion.

As fucking if.

I stood and paced.

Oh, I'd seen that crushed look on his face when I refused his bite. And since the moment Astra had *assigned* him to babysit me while I was on Rogue 5, I'd done my best to ignore him. It was hard to do so since it felt like he was devouring me, consuming me with his eyes until I had no secrets left. He already knew what I looked like naked, knew my scars existed, knew how I liked to fuck, what made me scream.

I wanted to shift and squirm under his scrutiny, but I

refused to let him see he affected me. The feeling persisted all through the journey to Rogue 5 and had evolved into something resembling fear—fear that he could see inside me somehow and read my mind. I wanted him. Wanted more of what we'd had, and I even started to think I might like his bite.

No. No! No biting!

Zenos moved from his spot beside Rhord to loom over me so that I could no longer pace. "No, you are not going anywhere."

His response annoyed me. He was only confirming what I'd already said, but his tone implied I had no choice in the matter. Which was also true, but he didn't need to know that. Then again, I didn't need to start a fight. But I did anyway. I couldn't help it with him. He riled me in so many ways, it seemed bickering was an outlet to all the sexual need I had for him. Better to argue than to fuck in front of the others. "You're mad because I didn't hand over the antidote," I argued.

"And you're mad because you are under *my* protection now. And you *will* obey me."

I pursed my lips. "As long as you don't get in my way."

"You will obey me, female." He pointed at me. "You are my responsibility."

I shrugged casually. "Not a big deal. I think you are just jealous the other guy was going to bite me."

"You are cruel to even ask it of him," he snarled.

Astra, Barek and Rhord—I'd learned his name when we'd boarded the ship—sat before us, one big guy on either side of her. All three were watching—or glaring, depending —as if they were at a tennis match, heads swiveling back and forth.

"We wouldn't be doing this right now if you'd just let

him bite me as proof," I tossed back, thumbing over my shoulder at Barek.

Zenos waved his hand, his finger almost touching my chest. "That's right, because you'd be dead."

I sighed but raised my voice hoping that maybe he'd understand the thing I'd been saying over and over if I spoke even louder. "I *told you* I took the antidote and you won't hurt me. If you'd just bite me, I'd be headed to Rogue 5 to track down the Quell dealer, you'd have your antidote and we'd never see each other again. Wouldn't that be fun?"

"If I bite you, if any one of us bites you, female, and you survive, you will never leave Rogue 5. You will be fucked and claimed and kept safe."

"Bullshit. I am not a toy or a possession."

"The bite is not a game. We mate for life. You ask Barek, a complete stranger, to sacrifice a future with another female for you? You told me you didn't want a mate. Have you changed your mind?" He flashed his fangs at me and my heart skipped a beat despite my best efforts to remain angry. God he was so damn hot. I did want his bite, and that was just not right. Not part of the plan.

"I am not staying. I am here to collect a bounty and avenge my friends. That is all."

"Rogue 5 is dangerous."

"I'm dangerous."

He laughed and crossed his arms over his chest. "You're delusional if you think Astra would just let you go to our legion without protection."

I smiled, rolled my eyes. He made me crazy. I wanted to punch him and kiss him at the same time. "Me, delusional? Yeah, and you're an asshole for not telling me who you were earlier."

"As I recall, you were not interested in talking."

Astra snapped her fingers, focusing our attention on her. "Both of you are behaving like children."

Zenos glared at me as if I'd insulted him by the mere act of breathing. As if I'd started this whole mess. He looked to Astra as if he'd forgotten she was there. His entire being seemed to be focused on me. Just me. The sensation was hypnotic, especially since all we did was bicker and argue. Or fuck.

I imagined what it might be like if he'd claimed me for real—for more than just a one-night stand or a quickie in an empty gaming room—his cock stretching me open, his fangs buried in my shoulder as he took me, claimed me, consumed me. And that mating fist thing...

I shivered. No. I couldn't go there, not with him standing so close to me that I could smell his skin. My pussy was still sore from our previous encounter. I hadn't used a ReGen wand to heal my tender, well-used flesh because, the truth was, I liked the soreness. It reminded me that I was alive. Human. That I could still feel something other than grief and loss. That I had contact with others, that I could engage. Belong. *Be.*

Perhaps that was why I was so pissed at him. He made me *feel*, and I hadn't done that in months.

I took a deep breath, let it out. "Fine," I snapped, sounding like a pouting teenager. "How much longer will we be on this ship?" I spun on my heel and directed my question to Astra, ignoring the hulking male who pushed every one of my buttons. My anger button and my clit—my favorite button of all for him to push. God, I was turning into a lunatic.

Zenos bristled behind me—I couldn't see him, but I could sense his displeasure at my blatant disregard—and I could hear him moving, which made Astra's gaze dart to him before returning to me. I ignored the sulking male because if she didn't want me to argue, I couldn't look at him. He riled me up, and the only way to get that aggression out was *not* happening on the shuttle and certainly wasn't happening while he was a bossy, know-it-all alpha male.

Astra smirked at me as if the question were amusing. It wasn't. "About an hour."

Sixty more minutes. Three thousand six hundred more seconds of Zenos breathing down my neck. Of making me want to give him a tongue lashing... or do something else to him with my tongue.

Aagh! Stupid hormones!

An hour was too damned long. I wasn't going to make it. "It's too crowded in here with his overinflated ego. I need some space."

Astra chuckled and the sound roamed over my skin like tiny needles grazing but not quite breaking through. With a sigh I turned and practically stalked out of the tiny gathering area that seemed to be their all-in-one dining room, talking room, sitting around doing nothing but waiting room. The ship wasn't small, but it wasn't a battleship either. I guessed it could hold fifteen or twenty fighters, of Atlan—or Rogue 5—size, but it seemed like there wasn't enough space. Not for me *and* Zenos.

The other hybrid, Nevuh—or Nev as they called him—piloted the ship. Why there weren't two of them up there in the cockpit like Coalition regulations, I didn't know, but the running of this team was Astra's business, not mine. All I had to do was get to Rogue 5 and find the drug-running scum responsible for the Quell that had brought down my friends.

I roamed the twelve feet of corridor, realized there was nothing on this ship but the all-in-one room, some very cramped barracks with beds stacked on top of each other like playing cards in a deck, the cargo area—which was about as welcoming as a dark, endless cave with a thousand spiders—and the cockpit. Nev hadn't struck me as obnoxious when we boarded, at least he didn't scowl at me every second like Zenos did, so I went there.

Astra appeared unconcerned with my whereabouts since there wasn't anywhere to go. Like an airplane on Earth, it wasn't like I was about to get off. They'd already stripped me of all my weapons, and I had to guess she wasn't worried about me taking down four hybrid Forsians with my bare hands. Which I had to admit, might be possible with my enhancements, but I doubted I'd survive. But she didn't know about me, about what I'd had to do to survive. Or what I'd chosen to do to live, and to hunt. She assumed I was normal. And if I were a standard issue human, the thought of me taking on all four of them would have been a joke.

I could fight when I had to, and I wasn't small, by Earth standards anyway, but I was still female and every one of these guys had about a foot of height and at least a hundred pounds on me. In their minds, if they took away my ship and my blasters, I was like every other human out in space, the underdog when it came to these huge aliens. Which meant humanity survived by ingenuity and our wits, and that was just fine with me. Except I had more. So much more they knew nothing about.

I was nearly to the cockpit, the closed door a few steps away, when a very large hand grabbed me by the elbow and spun me around.

"What kind of game are you playing, female?"

Even if the sound of that voice didn't make every feminine inch of me scream in recognition, I would have recognized his touch. Gentle. Even angry, his fingers moved over my arm in a caress. It was weird and creepy and kind of endearing all at once. Jeez, this guy tied me up in knots. Which was *exactly* why I hadn't wanted him to bite me back on the Transport Station Zenith. I was vulnerable to him, but I refused to let him know that.

"What do you mean?" I snapped, trying to shrug his palm off my shoulder. "I'm not playing any games." At least not with him. I was *avoiding* even a hint of any kind of game with him. And that was the truth.

I allowed him to turn me to face him, and when he took a step closer, I instinctively backed away until my shoulders met the cold, solid wall. I had to tilt my head up to meet his gaze. I licked my lips, swallowed a groan as I realized he could lift me up, wrap my legs around his hips and plunge deep. Hard. Right here, against the wall, like an animal. Just like back on Zenith.

"Do not look at me with lust in your eyes, female. I am responsible for your safety on Rogue 5. You are my problem now, and I will not have you taunting the others with your soft skin. You will *never* again ask for a hybrid's bite. Our venom might kill you. I will not allow it. If you ask and one of these idiots attempts to bite you, I will end him." His hands tightened on my shoulders. "Do I make myself clear?"

Well, well, well. He was serious. His gaze was almost as lethal as his bite. To others. I was impervious to both. I almost smiled at the sound of jealousy in his voice. Almost, because I wasn't stupid enough to go that far.

"You've told me all this before. You're like a broken record."

He frowned. "I do not know what that is. Regardless, it seems I need to repeat it again and again as you are not understanding."

"Yeah, a broken record."

Clearly, he was mad as hell... and hard as a rock. His cock was plainly evident beneath his pants, the heat of his flesh practically scorching me through my own uniform despite the fact that he held himself several inches away. The lack of contact made me crave him more. Why did we have to fight and want to fuck?

What I'd loved about him when we'd fucked earlier was his complete lack of control. Yes, he hadn't bitten me, so he'd been restrained, but other than that he'd been wild. Uninhibited. I'd loved it. Wanted more, even now. I wanted to push his buttons, make him lose it, just a little bit. Just *enough*, because for some stupid reason, I craved it.

Oh, I knew I was playing with fire, but I just couldn't help myself. He was so... *fuck*.

This man—alien—whatever, sent both my body and my imagination to naughty, naughty places. He'd fucked me on a game table and against a wall, my legs wrapped around his waist. What would it be like if he spun me about and pressed me into the cockpit door, fucked me from behind? Made me drop to my knees and suck his cock?

So many ideas came to mind, all of them making me wet. And horny.

I took my time, my gaze roaming over him slowly, admiring every inch. The sturdy legs with thighs like tree trunks. Narrow hips. Powerful abs. Broad shoulders. Strong jaw. When I got to his mouth, I licked my lips, and his gaze grew darker, his hands clenched into fists at his sides. His black gaze was penetrating. So hot it looked cold.

"I told you I only wanted one time, a quickie, Zenos. No games. No bullshit. *No biting*. Those rules were for you. Telling Barek to bite me wasn't to mess with you, it was to prove a point, not because I wanted to climb him like a tree."

"You want to climb a tree?"

I put my hands on my head, yanked on my hair, groaned.

"You, Zenos. You are the one with a problem here, the *only one*. This is about you. Not Barek. Our time together was just for fun. God, I didn't tell you my name for a reason."

"And what reason was that, Ivy?" He leaned in and placed his hands at either side of my head so I was caged, pinned. Under his control. And that fast my knees went weak and my pussy was wet and pulsing. God, this guy was lethal to my senses. "Are you working your way through all the hybrid Forsians? Trying to entice another into biting you... just a few hours later? Is it your intention to torment one of my brethren in front of me and risk your own life for your vengeance?"

Well, when he put it that way...

"I wasn't risking my life," I countered. "I *told* you that. The antidote keeps me safe, no matter what you think. No, I wasn't doing it to mess with your friends. For that I'm sorry." I paused, looked him in the eye so he could see I was sincere, at least about that. He might be jealous, but I wouldn't pit him against his friends. "And yes, I want vengeance. I need it. My friends are dead. They were my family, do you understand? *My family*. And they all died. Every. Single. One of them."

Gently now, he turned my face to the side and lifted my hair away from my exposed neck. Shivering at the intimate touch—how could a guy so dang big be so gentle?—I sighed when his fingertips traced the thick line of scar that began at the base of my skull and ran the back of my neck to disappear beneath my uniform. "And you were only injured?"

He had been able to connect what had happened to me

and the scar he'd seen, touched. I was *melting*. I sucked in a breath. Was it hot in here? "Yes." If nearly dying, making a deal with the devil and living to tell about it counted as *injured*.

"Why did a ReGen pod not take care of this?" His fingers continued to stroke my neck, but his gaze returned to mine. His touch was tender, but he would not release me without an answer.

"They didn't find me for almost two months. The scars were permanent by then."

"A surgeon could have removed them."

I shook my head. They were part of me, a reminder of what I'd lost and what I'd survived. "No. They stay."

"On Rogue 5 scars are badges of honor," he said.

"That's why you spoke of them, touched them earlier?"

He nodded, then stepped back, and the air around me went from inferno temperature to deep-space cold. I wanted him back, wanted to exist in that small space where I knew nothing could get to me, nothing could hurt me, and all because of Zenos. But that wasn't why I was here, on this ship. I had a job to do, a debt of blood and honor and love I owed to the friends I hadn't been able to save.

I took a deep breath and tried to get my head back on straight. "Is that all, Zenos? You wanted to tell me not to flirt with the others? I apologized."

"No." He crossed his arms now, and the glare was back. "I accept your apology, but I will also not allow you to risk your life like that again. To you, the act is professional, proof the antidote works. To us, biting is so much more. It *means* something. We've lived our entire lives knowing it was deadly. Forbidden. What you ask threatens to unleash something we've kept in check. Always."

I didn't mind poking Zenos's inner bear, but it was

unkind of me to mess with the others. I could see that now. I nodded. "I understand. I shall apologize to Barek if you wish."

"Good. Now, when we arrive, you will not go anywhere on Rogue 5 without me. Is that clear?"

The biting was one thing, but these other rules? We'd see about that once we landed, but for some inexplicable reason I couldn't make myself lie to him, so I remained silent.

"If you do not give me your word, I will tell Astra to turn this ship around and take you back the moment she has the antidote," he vowed.

"I don't like ultimatums," I countered. "This can be easily solved. I just won't give her the antidote."

He leaned in close, his lips grazing my cheek as he spoke. "Then she'll kill you on the spot." He lingered, inhaling, breathing me in. "She might be female, but she's not nice. She's the most ruthless among us. She'd have you tortured first. She'd break you, get the transport code and *then* kill you."

Shit. He was right. The moment I'd set foot on Astra's ship, she had all the cards. And I *would* break. I knew I would. I wasn't some kind of badass superhuman who could resist torture for days on end to protect an antidote I didn't really care all that much about. I might be super strong now, but there was only so much I could fight. The serum samples were a means to an end. A path to my vengeance. Nothing more.

To me. Nothing more to me.

To these aliens, that antidote was life. Mating. Children. Family. It was *everything.*

"I think I hate you, Zenos of Astra."

His eyes narrowed. "Give me your word, human. You will

not go anywhere alone, and you will not disobey me when your life is in danger."

I was not foolish enough to think I was going to win this battle. And like it or not, if I gave him my word, I would honor it. Damn him. "Fine," I snapped. "You promise no biting, and I agree I won't go anywhere without telling you—"

He raised his brows. "And you will not disobey me."

"And I won't disobey you *if my life is in danger*, but only while I'm under your protection. Once this is done, I owe you nothing."

"Agreed." He studied me closely, nodded, then walked away. I watched him until he disappeared back into the all-in-one room with the others. Unable to face him any longer, exhausted from arguing with him, I went to the cockpit and slumped down in the copilot's chair. Nev glanced my way but said nothing. The view was breathtaking. Stars. Galaxies. Colors I'd never imagined before I'd left Earth behind.

But I saw none of it, my mind replaying the scene in the corridor over and over and over until I wasn't sure if I wanted to rip that annoying male's clothes off his body or beat him bloody for being such an ass. I decided, after a while, that it was a bit of both.

enos, Personal Quarters, Astra Legion, Rogue 5

THE HUMAN WAS DRIVING me insane. I'd never wanted to strangle someone and fuck them in equal measure before. To make it even more frustrating, I couldn't fuck her the way I wanted. Wild. Hard. And with fangs.

"This is where you live?" she asked, looking around. The space wasn't fancy. Nothing on Astra was. We were simple people, content with simple things.

The moment we'd arrived, Astra had demanded the transport code. Ivy had rattled off the long string of coordinates like they weren't the most important bit of information Astra had acquired in years. The transport was initiated immediately, and the moment Barek had his hands on the vials, he handed one to Astra and took off for the lab like his flesh was on fire.

I knew what he wanted. He wanted to claim our leader. Bite her. Make her scream with pleasure. I wanted to do the same to Ivy, but taking what I wanted wasn't an option. Not until the antidote had been proven. And not if the female in question didn't want me in return. I'd seen how that worked out in the past, the way other foolish males had pursued mates who not only didn't want them but actively disliked them. They'd been good for a quick fuck but nothing more. The look in those females' eyes had been... well, not unlike the detached look Ivy had now.

She glanced around my quarters, but she saw nothing. Her mind was elsewhere. Plotting. Scheming. She'd upheld her end of the bargain, and she was preparing for the hunt. She wanted her bounty, this Gerian Eozara. I had no doubt if I didn't keep an eye on her, she'd head to Cerberus Legion right now. She would attempt to hunt on her own—as if she'd make it more than a few steps within that ruthless legion and survive—and that I could not allow.

She wasn't *mine,* but that didn't appear to matter to the instincts raging through my body, demanding I protect her —and not simply because Astra had ordered it. Because I could do nothing less. I would not see her hurt. I knew what anyone in the legion would do if they captured her. What their leader, Cerberus, could do, *would* do, if he got his hands on her.

Ivy may not know it, but Astra's ultimatum was protecting her. Keeping her safe.

Now I was stuck with her, the most complicated thing on all of Rogue 5. The other legions didn't share their secrets, but I would bet my right fang she was the only human on the moon base. One of the very few outsiders *not* from Rogue 5. Every other male or female from here to Hyperion were born and raised on the moon base. Knew the customs. The rules. The laws, said and unsaid.

She might have studied up on Rogue 5 as I would if I

were venturing to one of the pleasure resorts on Viken, learning the customs and geography of that green planet.

She knew *nothing* of Rogue 5. Not the real way of life. And she was my responsibility. Mine.

My cock considered the word *mine* in a completely different way. My cock wanted to mate her, to keep her forever, complete the claiming with the mating fist. If I truly made her mine, my cock would swell and lock me deep inside her, fucking her until we were both completely sated. My fangs wanted to pierce that sweet flesh, mark her so all could see she was beyond their reach.

And if I did both at the same time? She truly would belong to me, regardless of where she was from, why she was here or where she was going next.

There would be no going *anywhere* next. The thought of keeping her forever equally appealed to me and repelled me because the female who was walking around my space, taking in my small seating area, the eating area and the sleeping room with avid curiosity, pushed every emotional sore spot I had. Riled me in body, mind and soul.

"This is where I live," I said calmly. At least as calmly as possible with her.

"It's nice. I had even smaller quarters with the Coalition. Just enough space for a bed, and if I stuck my arms out, I could touch walls on both sides."

"This isn't the Coalition."

She turned to look at me. "I'm well aware we're not in Kansas anymore, Toto."

I frowned because she spoke in Earth slang... again. Stared. "I have no idea what that means."

She sighed. "It means... it means this place is different than what I'm used to."

I laughed, crossed my arms over my chest. "Everything

about Rogue 5 is different than what you're used to. Different than whatever a comm vid could share."

She faced me head-on, looked me over, just as she had in the canteen on Zenith. Her gaze stalled on the front of my pants, at the thick outline of my cock beneath the uniform. I had no idea why she made me so damn hard. Arguing with her should have made me soft, but sparring with her aroused me. Heated my blood. Filled my balls.

"Not everything is different."

I shook my head. "Do you claim that you're used to the fucking I gave you? I do not believe you have been taken by a male like me before."

"True. You're the only one who's had fangs."

"I'm the only one who's made you come screaming. Made you lose control."

Her hands went to her hips, and her cheeks turned pink. "You're so full of yourself."

I took a step toward her. She didn't retreat. Didn't even blink. She was so fucking fierce and defiant. So willful. I wanted to take her over my knee and spank that sass right out of her, but then again, my cock liked her wild and untamed. She might not be from Rogue 5, but she had the passion of one of us.

"No, *you'll* be full of *me* in just a minute."

She sputtered, rolled her eyes.

She fucking rolled her eyes.

"I don't think so."

I didn't reply right away, just looked her over. Highlighted by the tight outlines of her modified Coalition uniform, I couldn't miss the way her breathing had sped up or that her nipples jutted out through the thick fabric. I couldn't scent her arousal as an Everian or hybrid Everian might, but I didn't need to scent her body to know she was wet.

She got off on this. She liked it when I pushed her. Challenged her. Made her bend.

"Tell me, Lieutenant, what happened when you contradicted your superior officers like you are doing with me."

Her lips pressed into a thin line. Yeah, she hated being called by her former rank.

"I was punished. KP or shuttle cleaning." The words were laced with distaste, and I had no doubt she'd suffered such punishments often.

"I spank."

"What?" she sputtered.

"You're my responsibility here on Rogue 5. That means if you disobey me, you get your tight ass spanked. And you know why you'll submit to it?"

Her gaze narrowed, but I saw the pink flush to her cheeks, the gleam of interest and heat in her gaze.

"Why?" she gritted out.

"Because unlike shuttle cleaning, you're going to enjoy the burning sting of my hand on your ass."

"I'm not going to like anything that has to do with you."

I grinned then. "See? You're intentionally being contrary because you *want* to know what I'll do. You want to feel my heated palm on your ass. You want a little bite of pain with your pleasure."

Her mouth opened and closed then. I'd stunned her silent. I took the moment to end this and take it where we both wanted to go.

To bed.

I stalked over to her, leaned forward and into her belly so I could toss her over my shoulder. While she wasn't small for a female, especially a human one, she was much smaller than me. She was light, and I didn't break step as I carried her into the sleeping room. Dropped her onto the bed.

She bounced once and popped back up. With a hand to her chest, I pressed her down.

"Here's how this is going to go," I said.

She fumed, her eyes shooting fire at me. I loved it, at least here in my quarters. She was contained, all her energy aimed at me. Angry because I was right. Angry because she wanted to follow my orders. Oh, it bucked against every bit of her rebellious nature. She wouldn't admit it, but she wanted me to prove myself more powerful. Strong enough to protect her. Rule her. Sate her.

Needed that reassurance from me.

She wouldn't respond with words. Indeed I had no doubt she would argue with me if I told her there was no oxygen in deep space.

She'd believe my actions though. And she would learn to trust me. Perhaps not the first time, but I was willing to teach this particular lesson again and again.

My cock agreed with this. She wanted to challenge me? To play? To push me so I would dominate her? She'd get what she wanted. She would surrender. Eventually.

We'd both find pleasure in every bit of her resistance and in her final submission.

"Fuck you," she snarled.

"I think you mean I'll fuck you. In about two minutes my cock will be inside you. We just need to set a few ground rules first."

She pushed up onto her elbows, but my hand wasn't allowing her to rise any higher. I loomed over her, but the sight of her on my bed, panting, fuming and fucking gorgeous was something I'd never forget.

"Rules? I left the Coalition to avoid rules."

"Astra said we will search out those responsible for the Quell problem tomorrow. The specific Cerberus member, Gerian Eozara. Tomorrow," I repeated. "Until then we will stay in my quarters. Word is being spread that you belong to me, at least here on Rogue 5. If that is the case, then we may as well reap the rewards, don't you think?"

"What rewards do I get being stuck with you?"

"My mouth. My fingers. My cock. Orgasms."

"So cocky."

"You know it's true. You received firsthand proof when you got all those things from me. This time we have a bed and much longer."

"We can't stand each other," she snapped.

I didn't hate her. She was everything I had ever wanted in a mate but couldn't have. She was the tastiest treat that I couldn't truly savor. My fangs dropped, and I wanted to sink them into her just as I had done with my cock, as I would again.

But the bite? No. It was impossible. I thought of the Earth term she'd mentioned. I was like a broken record. I wouldn't risk her life.

I stood at the edge of the bed, tugged off my shirt. "We only dislike each other when we have clothes on. Strip."

She remained propped up on her elbows and watched me take off my clothes. I didn't mind if she did so. Earlier on Zenith we hadn't taken time to explore, to savor each other's bodies. I wanted her to know what I offered, what she'd get from me. My body belonged to her. My cock, now free of pants, aimed right at her.

She would receive everything but the fangs.

"Take off your clothes, or I'll take them off for you," I ordered.

Her eyes narrowed again, but she must have realized arguing wasn't going to get her body what it craved. Hot, sweaty fucking. Orgasms. Pleasure.

Shifting around, she moved up onto her knees, removed her shirt and bra. She fell backward onto the bed and worked off her pants. I helped her by leaning forward and tugging off her boots.

"That wasn't too bad, was it?"

Her gaze was affixed on my cock. "What are you talking about?"

"Obeying. If you behave yourself, you'll get what you want."

"And you know what I want?"

"You know I do."

She said nothing in response, only moved her foot across the bed, spreading her legs wider so I could see all of her. *All.*

Her knees fell open in silent invitation. She wouldn't say what she wanted, couldn't give in to that. But she showed me. Fuck, did she.

I grinned.

Reaching out, I gripped one ankle, twisted my wrist so she flipped over onto her belly. I knelt on the bed, dropped my palm onto her ass, watched the lush flesh bounce. Watched my handprint bloom pink.

She gasped at the action, looked over her shoulder at me.

If looks could kill...

I slid my hand over her pussy, felt how wet she was. Everything that had happened since we fucked in the empty game room had been foreplay for this.

She was hot. She was wet. She was ready. Oh, I wanted to play with those perfect breasts, suck on the pink tips. I wanted to finger her pussy until she came. Lick her clit until she screamed. Work a finger into her ass and see how much she begged for more.

I wanted all of that, fuck, did I.

But she'd have my cock first. I crawled up between her thighs, spread them wide before circling my arm about her waist and pulling her back so she was up on her knees. I didn't wait, only gripped the base of my cock and aligned it with her entrance, the wet, tight core that I couldn't forget.

I thrust deep, filled her in one long, hard stroke.

Her fingers gripped the bedding as her head came back. She cried out at the force of my cock's invasion. Her pussy clenched and milked my cock as she adjusted, her wet welcome coating me. My balls were covered with her juices, and when I pulled back, the sounds of wet, messy sex filled the air.

I could scent her now, thick and sweet.

"More?" I taunted.

"More," she replied immediately.

It was just as I'd thought. This was the one way we were completely compatible. Completely perfect. Completely attuned.

Everything fell away. Astra. The Coalition. The bounty. Quell. The antidote. All of it.

This was pure instinct. Basic. Primitive. Perfect.

The only thing I couldn't do was bite. I could resist. I would, for her. She was too important to risk, too beautiful to hurt. Too fucking perfect.

As I fucked her for the second time, I knew there would be no one better suited for me. *We* were perfect. Together.

My handprint was bright and fierce on her pale skin, making my balls draw up. I was ready to come, but I didn't want to see her ass or watch the way my cock disappeared inside her when I filled her with my seed.

No, I wanted to see her face, to watch her as she came. And so I pulled out. She all but snarled at me for taking away her pleasure. I flipped her easily and sank back into her.

I was so much taller I had to arch my back to meet her gaze.

"Ivy," I said, my voice ragged, my hips losing the steady rhythm for a cadence that came from nature, driving me to take her hard and fast until I came, until I pumped all my cum into her. Marked her. Scented her so everyone would know she was mine. No bite, but a well-fucked female was obvious to all on Rogue 5.

"What?" she gasped, closed her eyes.

"You'll come when I do."

Her head moved back and forth on the bed. "I can't hold off."

"You will."

Her eyes opened, and she stared at me, ready to argue with stinging words. Instead all that came out was a gasp as I altered the angle of my hips and rubbed over her clit.

I couldn't hold back, not with the way her inner muscles were rippling around me, how she got wetter from my two-word command.

"Now." I gritted my teeth, snarled my pleasure as I came, pumping all of me into her. The way she did exactly as I'd said and came with me increased the intensity of my release. Our orgasms merged, our breaths tangled, our hearts pounded.

We were one in this moment, in total accord. Nothing would be more perfect except the bite. The mating fist that locked me to her.

As I caught my breath, I realized I did not need those things to be satisfied with her. For while we would not be caught together for hours as the mating fist would ensure, as a formal claiming required, we could fuck again. And again. All night long.

Ivy tangled her foot in my leg and lifted her hips. She flipped us. I allowed it—I was too big for her to do so against my will—so she was on top. Her body lowered on mine, her pussy a hot, wet clamp that tightened around my still-hard cock, dragging a moan of pleasure from me as she took me deeper, ground her ass against my groin.

"Again," she said.

I smiled, well pleased.

I'd been right. We were perfect for each other.

As long as I didn't bite. As long as I could keep myself from accidentally killing her.

7

Ivy, Astra Legion, Rogue 5

"HOW MUCH CAN ONE PERSON EAT?" I sat across from Zenos and watched the giant male consume more food over the course of an hour than I could eat in a week. Not that I was complaining. My body was sated, my stomach was full and I wore brand-new Astran armor. I'd been given a green armband, signifying the Astra Legion, but had accidentally left it in Zenos's room when he bent me over bathroom sink and fucked me from behind. A girl couldn't complain about that reason.

I'd dropped the uniform I was putting on and the armband must have been kicked under my old clothes. It didn't matter since we were going back to his room for weapons before we started the hunt. I'd grab it then. Either way it didn't appear to matter to anyone in the room, unlike with the Coalition. Everyone—and everything—had to be perfect all the time.

The uniform, with its odd markings, appeared to be enough to convince the people here to trust me, or the fact that I was with Zenos, the hybrid eating machine. There was no doubt they could tell I was an outsider. In a weird way I felt like I was in a bar on the wrong side of the tracks, so completely different, but Astrans trusted each other's judgments. If Zenos gave me a uniform and was with me, then I was in. People didn't question, and I liked that. Respected it. I wasn't getting any special attention or stares from the handful of families eating here. I was, in a sense, one of them.

For now.

Why that thought nearly brought me to tears, I didn't understand and had no desire to examine more closely. I didn't belong here on Rogue 5, not really. Or with Zenos. He knew I had taken the antidote and had filled me with his cock but *still* refused to bite me—not that I wanted a mate—and as soon as this bounty hunt was done, I was out of here. Gone. Like the wind. It wasn't the mate thing that pissed me off, but the biting thing. He could bite me while his cock wasn't in me. It would hurt, but I imagined the exquisite pleasure that would follow. They wouldn't be so eager to do so if it wasn't driven by orgasm. They weren't ruthless animals. We were all alike in that, pushed to achieve that incredible feeling in fucking someone else.

He denied himself that—and me—because he didn't trust me. That hurt most of all. Coalition fighters had to trust each other with their lives. The Astrans around me trusted each other, trusted Zenos to have someone accompany him who was not a threat or danger.

But Zenos trusting me? Nope.

It was all just pretend. Fake. Temporary.

"I like your hair down." Zenos shoved more food into his

mouth with an unapologetic grin. I sighed and turned in my seat to look around.

Yes, I'd left my hair down instead of putting it up in the usual braid or ponytail that meant business. He'd commented on how he liked to look at the *mesmerizing golden waves* after he'd made me come all over his cock this morning. And much as I couldn't quite believe I had done it, it turned out I was a romantic at heart after all.

I'd liked his words. Was pleased by them. Felt... dare I even think it? Pretty.

Apparently, I was vain, and I wanted him admiring me for as long as possible before we had to hunt. Admiring me. Wanting me. But trusting? I didn't think that was possible.

Maybe he'd even tell me I was beautiful...

Because of this, my hair was down for the first time in so long I could barely remember it being left untamed. And there was a lot of it, falling to my waist like a blonde curtain.

Enough thinking about my stupid hair. What was happening to me? I got a little bit of action between the sheets—and against the wall, in the bathing room—and I turned into the kind of woman who worried about her *hair*? Who took something that was just simple fucking and analyzed the hell out of it like a high school cheerleader?

No. Not going there. I focused on the now, where we were eating. It wasn't a cafeteria, exactly, but it wasn't grandma's kitchen either. The room was smallish, big enough for maybe thirty people to sit and eat at any given time. Since I was bored—I'd finished my meal what felt like eons ago—and nervous to hit Cerberus Legion, and so impatient to have the asshole who had sold the Quell to my unit in my grasp, I couldn't just sit and stare any longer. I tapped my foot. Counted chairs.

Two, four... ten. Twenty. Thirty-four. About half of them empty. Damn, I was good.

"Why don't you have an armband on? You're gonna get in trouble. Astra can't keep you safe if you don't wear it every day. That's what my mom says. Did you forget it in your room?"

"What?" I turned toward the small voice and discovered two little ones staring up at me with wide, curious eyes and absolutely no fear. The little girl was about five—assuming these Rogue 5 hybrids aged the same way human children did—and who I assumed was her younger brother, perhaps three. Close in age. Their dark brown hair, copper-toned skin and slightly angular features reminded me of the Prillon warriors I'd battled with in the Coalition Fleet. Prillon hybrids perhaps? Whatever they were, they were adorable, and so were the tiny fangs just visible when she smiled at me. A big, open, trusting smile. Prillon with fangs. What a ruthless combination, and yet in such adorable little packages.

So innocent. With *fangs*. God, I was obsessed with the stupid fangs.

"Why don't you have your armband on?" she repeated.

I cleared my throat and looked at Zenos for guidance. What was I supposed to say? I'd been too busy having sex to keep track of it? It got lost when the big hybrid Forsian seated across from me took me from behind? Yeah, neither of those would work. Zenos raised a brow and stuffed another bite of food into his mouth. Really helpful.

"Well, I forgot it in my room," I said finally, offering her a small smile. There wasn't much opportunity to hang out with kids in the Coalition. Sure, some lived on the big battleships with their families, but I hadn't really had contact with any of them. I'd been on the smaller crafts, just fighters waiting or being sent to battle. On Earth none of my friends had had kids yet, and I'd been an only child. I didn't dislike children, I just hadn't had much contact with them. Out of sight, out of mind, pretty much.

She smiled and pulled her little brother by the arm, tucking him in closer to her side. He went, without complaint, which was damn adorable. "I'm Scylla and my brother is Nero."

"Nice to meet you both. I'm Ivy."

She nodded as if this was not new information, as if word of me had spread even to the preschool crowd.

"My mother says you are mated to Zenos now." She rocked back and forth on her heels, her eager face glowing with excitement. I had no idea what to say, but she kept talking. I looked about the room, wondered who her mother was. Why was she letting her kids come up to a stranger? Were there no worries here within Astra? It seemed not. Zenos didn't worry, he kept shoveling in the food. "He is my favorite when we play giants and pirates. He makes the best noises." Her face lit up with glee, and she clapped her hands together.

"Who?"

"Zenos. The best giant of them all."

"What?" Giants and pirates? Zenos?

A loud roar came from Zenos, and I startled, so shocked, the sound bouncing off the walls of the room like a cannon blast. *Like a giant.*

My ass hit the floor, the kiddos laughed like I was the funniest thing they'd ever seen and Zenos stood over all of us looking a bit too satisfied with himself, arms crossed over his chest. Grinning.

I looked around quickly, but the other Astra adults in the room grinned or ignored us completely, as if this was a common scene. Zenos played with kids. Kids went up to strangers. I wasn't a stranger, I was with Zenos. And he wasn't just a big, brawny guy from Rogue 5 that liked to push my buttons and fuck me hard. He was also a huge softy. Who knew? Definitely not me.

I hadn't been prepared for that roar. I'd been too comfortable, too relaxed, which could have been the result of multiple orgasms. Now I was on the floor looking like an idiot—and my backside needed a good rubbing. I'd have to be prepared for that next time, to not let my guard down so much. The roar or any kind of enemy. I was too complacent, which made me scowl. Rattled, I messed with my hair, which was so fifteen-year-old-girl behavior. Another reason I didn't leave it down. Frustrated, I gathered the long strands and swept the mess up over my shoulder to the front.

Scylla gasped. "Oh! Can I touch them?"

"What?" I asked... again. My hair? We all had hair, mine wasn't anything special. But God, could I say anything else to the small child but *what*?

Zenos's playful grin had faded, and he looked at the two children with a grave expression.

"Ivy does not understand our ways yet, little one, but as you can see, she is a very strong warrior."

His words sank in, making me feel warm and tingly and far too happy. Zenos thought I was strong, even with my ass on the floor? He didn't even know the truth yet, the truth about my past, my injuries, the scars he said were special, what I'd done to survive...

"Can I? Can I touch them?" Scylla's eyes glowed, and she practically danced and wiggled around like she was either overexcited or had to pee.

Touch what? I looked up to Zenos for help as Nero climbed into my lap and parked there on my thighs as if I were his mother and he belonged in my lap. Like he was mine.

It was as if I was sitting with him at story time at the library or something. It was a swift and ridiculous idea. A dangerous, dangerous thought, that one. He wasn't mine, and this definitely wasn't preschool hour. I looked around again, searching for their parents. *Rescue me!*

"Oh, um... okay," I said when no one stepped forward.

Completely at a loss as the tiny boy cuddled into me with a contented sigh, I looked from Nero to his dancing sister to the male staring down at me with a look in his eyes I'd never seen before. Gentle. Tender.

Proud.

"She wants to touch your scars, Ivy," Zenos said. "As I told you, they are a mark of honor and strength within Astra Legion. If you doubted me, you can believe a small child, hmm? Only the strongest among us survive with such scars. The most trusted. The bravest. The protectors among us."

My scars? "You were serious? Really? But they're on my back. She can't even see..."

A small hand settled at the base of my neck, and I stilled as she traced the line of my scar over my shirt, top to bottom.

I gasped and Zenos explained. "Our uniforms are designed to pick up the markings on our skin and display them." He pointed to his own arm and the odd assortment of marks and lines on his uniform that I'd always assumed was some kind of camouflage or intentional design. It was in the new clothing we'd donned earlier, not the other garments. Perhaps only here on Rogue 5 did they wear it, for I doubted anyone they met on Zenith had the same custom.

"It's a setting in the new uniforms," he said, validating

my thoughts. "Every scar is tracked by the suit and displayed as a badge of strength."

"What doesn't kill you makes you stronger," I murmured.

I quoted the famous Earth saying as the little girl inspected me from head to toe, touching me everywhere with no self-consciousness at all. Arms. Shoulders. Legs. Obviously a curious little thing, when she reached the top of my uniform, she moved my hair aside so she could track the scar all the way up to the base of my skull.

"Wow. You are *very* brave. Did that hurt?" she asked.

"Yes." The word was barely audible. Memory flashed through me like acid, and my breath caught in my throat, trapped there as the unexpected flash of horror held me paralyzed. I remembered the day my entire unit died, still wondered why I had not gone into the final dark with them. The images of that time crowded into my mind as if I had a horror film playing on repeat in my mind. I could still see the Hive Scout who'd sliced me open, feel the burning agony as my commander had pulled me through the dirt and gore before he'd died. The silence that had remained after they'd all succumbed still haunted me when I tried to sleep. I could see the surgeon, hear the crackling voice of the doctor who'd offered to make me more than what I was before, who gave me the illegal implants, who saved my life and gave me purpose.

I'd spent two months in that filthy clinic on the outskirts of the sector. Two months of agony as I fought to survive despite the knowledge that they were dead. My friends. The only people I loved in this universe. Dead. Every. Last. One.

"Ivy?" Zenos's voice sounded far, far away, like an echo.

The dining room in Astra Legion was gone. I was lost in my head, surrounded by death. Agony.

Pounding. All I could hear was the pounding of my blood through my ears. And screams. I covered my ears with my palms.

"Zenos's mate." Small. Innocent. So trusting. Nero brought me back to reality with a tug on my wrists and soft words.

Blinking, I pushed the memories back like I'd done thousands of times before. I blushed furiously, realizing what had happened. I dropped my hands to gently lift him from my lap. He went without protest, and I pushed myself to my feet to look down at both him and the little girl. She looked unsure now, and I hated myself for that. One more thing to add to the list. I gave her a small smile of reassurance. "Yes, honey, it hurt. A lot. But I'm okay now."

"Because you are strong." She nodded as if it were fact. She knew about scars, knew they were wounds that hurt, but nothing more complex than that. Thank God. A child's mind was so innocent of danger. Her smile was a relief, and I reached out to touch her soft cheek. She really was beautiful.

"Yes." I was, and it was time to start acting like it. To get my head back in the fucking game. Enough mooning over an alien male I couldn't have. Enough feeling safe, feeling cared for. The clothing didn't mean I truly belonged. It meant I wasn't naked. And my hair... God. Who could fight with long tresses getting in the way? Maybe in a Hollywood movie, but this was real. This was Rogue 5. I was such an idiot. Enough.

I shifted my gaze to Zenos, crossed my arms over my chest. "Playtime's over. Let's go. I have a job to do. It is time to find Gerian Eozara."

He lingered for a few moments to say goodbye to the children, but I couldn't watch. I didn't want to see him with them, didn't need that image in my mind of Zenos as the big, loving protector. As a father. As more than just the guy I fucked, because if I thought about him in any way but a giant orgasm machine, I might start to care. And that was the most dangerous thing of all.

And the game, giants and pirates? I wasn't either of those things. I wasn't a princess. I wasn't a hybrid. Hell, if I were perfectly honest, I wasn't exactly human anymore either. I had the scars to prove it. I was a bounty hunter, and it was time to stop living in a dreamland of happily ever after and babies and get back to work.

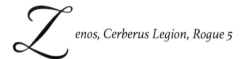

enos, Cerberus Legion, Rogue 5

IVY MOVED like a ghost through the streets, the dark black of our uniforms making it easy for the two of us to blend into shadows as we moved through enemy territory. She'd put her hair into a tight braid, and I missed the soft fall of gold down her back. I'd removed my armband—Ivy had yet to find hers—and reset our armor when we left the relative safety of the Astra-controlled region of the city. Nothing marked us now. We were truly rogue. And the outward display lines of Ivy's scars were gone as well. I missed them, wanted to strip her of her uniform and trace the lines with my tongue. To revel in her life experiences, her bravery. Her strength. To hear the full story of how she'd achieved them. Hold her if that was hard to do. Outward scars were one thing, internal ones, the demons we fought in our heads, was another.

"Keep up or I'm leaving you behind."

Her hissed warning made me grin, made my balls ache to master her again. Fierce, my female. But I'd seen the horror fill her eyes when little Scylla asked about the scars, knew there was a story. Devastation so deep the memories took her someplace hidden in her head at a simple mention. I'd very much needed to know what had made her shudder with fear and pain, needed to know everything about the female I became more obsessed with each passing moment. Needed to know who to kill for hurting her.

Scars were a sign of all we survived, but it was possible that was all Ivy had done. *Survived.* Pushing herself forward through time, but was she really living?

As hard as I tried, I couldn't get the image of little Nero curled up in her lap out of my mind. Couldn't stop imagining that it was my son or daughter she held instead. *Our* child. I'd never had such thoughts before, never gave myself a moment to even consider it, the idea too dangerous to my psyche. It held too much hope. Too much want for something I couldn't have.

Ivy had looked shocked when Nero placed himself in her care, as if kids were a novelty for her. She'd said she'd been a fighter for four years. That was a long time in battle and most likely without the simple comforts of a home, of family. I wondered who or what she'd left behind on Earth. Obviously she didn't long to return, for she'd laughed at Astra when she'd mentioned it. But four years without kin. Without connection to familial roots... She shrugged it off. Gods, she shrugged off everything, every emotion, and I had to wonder if it was because it hurt too much. If she felt *too* much.

I saw past that, to the tender side of her, one she probably didn't reveal often, even to herself or anyone else, and never to me. I'd seen her glare, snarl and stand toe-to-

toe with both Barek and Astra. I'd seen her gasping with pleasure. I'd seen lust and hunger and rage—but never *that*.

Gentleness. Caring.

Love, perhaps? Or at least the stirrings of emotions I had begun to fear she might not ever reveal. I'd taken her body. Fucked her. Filled her. Made her scream with pleasure. It was an escape for her. A way to retreat from the horrors that drove her. A short connection with another, a few moments of bliss found only in orgasm. Yet she had never looked at me with such softness, and I was shocked to discover I longed for her to bestow that gift upon me. Seeing her come on my cock, on my mouth was one thing. I wanted all of her, not just the prickly, argumentative facade she had firmly in place.

"What's wrong with you?" Ivy stood with her hands on her hips. She'd stopped moving and stood in the shadow of an awning, glaring at me as my mind had wandered. "Well? Are you *trying* to get us both killed?"

Yeah, this was the side of Ivy she showed me, *gave* me. Nothing more. I had to wonder if it was just me she refused to offer all of herself or if it was everyone. If she were hiding. Protecting herself from more than just the Gerian Eozara's of the universe.

Footsteps.

Grabbing her around the waist, I put my hand over her mouth and pressed her back against a door within a small, recessed archway. Shielded her with my body. Her eyelids narrowed, but she must have heard the group of young Cerberus males stomping past the end of the alley like a herd of wild beasts. They were arguing, drunk. Dangerous. They assumed they had nothing to fear. I had no doubt they were all armed and spoiling for either a good fuck or a bloody fight. Probably both. It was what they did while spending free time. Relaxation and carefree amusement meant carousing, throwing a few punches, drinking too much alcohol, a hard fuck.

Ivy nipped my palm with her teeth, just hard enough to get my attention, and I slowly lowered my hand. I narrowed my eyes. "Quiet. We don't want to draw their attention."

"No kidding, there are eight of them," she whisper-yelled.

I didn't know how she knew that specifically, as we'd been inside the archway, hidden from view, when they passed. Her chest heaved, her thighs pressed to mine, the moldable armor covering us both not nearly thick enough to prevent me from feeling every curve of her soft flesh against me as she scolded me some more. It was as if we were back in that empty room on Transport Station Zenith. Others could come upon us, the danger of being discovered the same. Now we had our clothes on, although my cock punched against my pants to get out, to get to Ivy. To get *in* her. Even now, when danger threatened just around the corner, I still longed to fuck her.

"I heard them half a block back," she snapped. "What were you doing back there? Taking a mental break? Get your head on straight or you're going to get us both killed."

She was right, but fuck me, I couldn't stop being distracted. She felt good, she smelled good. I knew she *tasted* good. Her sass made me hard, made me want to change her tone from argumentative to agreeable. I needed her hot, wet pussy wrapped around my cock, needed to hear her scream my name, needed to see her eyes glaze with pleasure. I needed her to lose control. Surrender. To me. Only to me.

My fangs erupted from my mouth, and I groaned, pushing forward, rubbing my hard cock against her so she'd know exactly how she affected me. "Ivy Birkeland from

Earth, you tempt me. Drag me to the center of Cerberus Legion and are contrary no matter the situation. I'm going to make you scream my name when this is over," I promised. "I'm going to fuck you until you beg for mercy, beg me to stop, and then I'm going to suck your sensitive clit into my mouth and make you come again."

I watched as her eyes flared, but it was quickly banked. Oh yes, she wanted it just as rough and wild as I.

"No biting?" she asked.

Why the fuck did she keep bringing that up? Again and again. She got my cock; she got my fingers and mouth and all the orgasms she wanted. Why did she continue to push?

By the fucking gods, did she *want* to die? "You know I cannot."

Yeah, every bit of emotion shuttered, and I felt her body slump against mine as if her motivation and desire had fled from one breath to the next. "Right."

She stared up at me, her bright blue eyes like deep pools of water whose depths I could not breach. And they'd gone cold as ice. "Well, if you want to fuck me later, we should probably keep moving now. Get this done. Astra's informant said we would find the crew I'm looking for about two blocks from here in a dive bar."

I frowned.

"What is a dive bar?" The establishment most Cerberus were known to frequent, and hopefully Gerian Eozara as well, served drugs and alcohol in equal measure, but no diving was involved.

She pushed me off her, waved her hand nonchalantly. "Never mind. Let's just go." Ivy slid out from between me and the wall, gliding smoothly from my arms and moving back into the dark alley. The small corridors on the moon base had been here from the early days. We were in the oldest sections of Rogue 5, once the heart of the moon settlement, but now they were a seedy underbelly, used for moving supplies and equipment, the ugly things people did not want to see.

Ugly things like me. Dangerous to not just the darkest elements of Rogue 5, but to the most innocent. My fangs were just as deadly as the ion blaster at my hip.

Hands clenched into fists, I pulled back from the archway and followed. Ivy moved quickly now, gaining ground on me at a pace that seemed impossible for a human. How did she move so fucking fast? Everian blood? Was she a Hunter? Impossible.

"Ivy, stop," I barked at her, but she kept moving, flowing like black water between pools of shadow. Her focus was unwavering, her intent plain. I had no idea humans were so agile. No wonder the Coalition Fleet was so pleased with the new planet and placed fighters from Earth on their ReCon teams. I had never fought with the Coalition, but all soldiers were the same once they arrived at the Transport Station Zenith. A few drinks at the bar and they liked to talk. I'd heard plenty of stories from and about humans as the visitors to Zenith relived their glories and defeats. Bragging. Hiding their pain behind laughter and their drug of choice, whether that was sex, alcohol or other, more potent and mind-numbing options... like Quell. They never spoke much of Earth, though, as if they were too homesick to bring it up or they didn't care.

I knew why Ivy hated that particular drug with such a violent obsession, knew that her unit had been high on Quell—and some kind of hallucinogen—when the Hive attacked. So I wondered what drug Ivy preferred, how she dealt with her pain. The moment the question formed in my mind, I knew the answer. Sex. She used sex to soothe the ache, to forget. A mindless fuck in a storage closet with a stranger from Rogue 5.

I'd been her drug. I still *was* her way to forget, to let go for even a short time. I performed a service for her.

But was fucking enough? It didn't seem like it, as if every time she returned to herself after an orgasm, she also returned to her memories, to everything that haunted and drove her to this place. They were so powerful for her she'd been willing to bargain with the leader of a Rogue 5 legion, to sneak into the center of the deadliest one without breaking a sweat.

I wondered if she had nightmares. Did she dream? Did humans dream? We'd slept beside each other the night before, but she'd been still. Or I'd been so soundly asleep I hadn't awoken to them. These questions made me realize I knew next to nothing about my little human. I wanted it all with her. Not just children like Scylla or Nero, but answers. Feelings. I wanted *emotion*. Connection in more than just sex.

Moving with speed I normally saved for battle, I caught up to my female. "Do humans dream?" I asked.

She glared up at me over her shoulder. "What are you talking about?"

"Do humans have visions while they sleep?" I asked, pressing the issue.

"You're asking me that here? Now?"

I didn't say anything, only waited.

She sighed. Confusion was clear in her wrinkled brow, but I saw a spark of curiosity as well. She glanced about, then answered. "Yes, humans dream."

"Do you?"

One blink and the ice was back. "Yes. I do."

She turned away from me, this discussion over, and

darted into another deep shadow, stopping to survey the area in front of us. Our destination was ahead, across the small street. True to its reputation, a large group of Cerberus scum gathered outside.

The front of the building had been torn down and replaced with reflective screens that showed popular vid feeds Rogue 5 had stolen and rerouted to our moon. One large display showed lush, green fields of grasses, trees and flowers, the word *Atlan* displayed along the edges. I wasn't sure if it was there to make those in this legion want to go to that planet or to hate them more for such a beautiful home world.

Another was a live feed of the founders' camp on planet Hyperion below us, where a few of our hybrids still traveled to maintain trade and relations with the brutish half of our ancestry. A well-known Prillon female sang a haunting melody on another screen as a brutal execution was broadcast live from Xerima on the next. It was hard to watch, and I quickly looked elsewhere. Fucking barbarians.

There were ten screens in all, a mix of beauty and brutality I had become accustomed to. It was Rogue 5, this dichotomy. It was life, although here in the thick of the Cerberus Legion, it was especially brutal. It made the sweet faces of Scylla and Nero all the more innocent. A reminder of why we were here now.

"What do you think?" Ivy asked, not the least bit interested in the displays. She glanced up at me over her shoulder but didn't linger long, her attention drawn back to the crowd.

I scanned our surroundings again. "At least ten inside, six outside. And that's only what we can see."

"That's what I counted as well." She reached down to her side and patted her weapons. Astra had relented and given her back her blasters since they were her weapon of choice. The Coalition standard, what she was comfortable and skilled at using. Ivy had managed to pick up another knife or two somewhere along the way. She was resourceful, I had to give her that.

"Sixteen is too many. And we don't know if Gerian Eozara is in there." I glanced around as if one of them would have a sign that offered up his name as our target. Out of all of Ivy's intel, she didn't know the appearance of Gerian Eozara.

"We should backtrack and find an escalation point for the rooftop." I pointed to the top of a building that would give us an excellent view of the area. A way to scan and assess the situation before moving in. "Watch and wait until we know he is there."

"Sixteen." She sighed and turned, pressing her back to the cold, dark side of the building. She didn't sound fearful, she sounded oddly relieved. "Is Astra going to be mad if we kill some of them?"

Was she serious? Surely not. "I'm here to keep you alive, Ivy. We are *not* going in there." I wasn't afraid but smart. "I can kill them all, but I can't fight sixteen and protect you at the same time."

She raised her brows and gave a quick, annoyed shake of her head. "You didn't answer the question."

"The answer is no. Astra won't be mad. Cerberus is our enemy, and we are not wearing legion colors; therefore we are rogue and killing some of them is not a problem."

"What if we were wearing the green armband?" she wondered, glancing at my upper arm.

I grinned. "Then this would be seen as an attack between legions. It would start a war."

The difference was slim but on Rogue 5, enough.

Armband, no armband. War versus plain killing.

"They'll know we came from Astra. Only Astra has all you big hybrid Forsian guys, right?"

How the hell did she know that? It wasn't as if I could blend in with this crowd. I didn't even look like a hybrid Atlan, I was so big. "That is correct. And yes, they will know." I looked down at where my armband usually rested. "As I said, if we are not wearing Astra's colors, we are acting on our own."

"I don't mind going rogue. I have for months now." She arched a pale brow. "It's ridiculous you guys can go around killing each other as long as you aren't actually wearing your legion's armband."

I nodded. "That's correct."

"That's stupid. It's still you." She looked me over, head to toe. "Everyone still knows it's you. That you're a hybrid Forsian. That you're from Astra Legion."

"And anyone getting a glimpse of you will know you are not from here, that you are human. It doesn't matter though. This isn't the Coalition. We're not even on a Coalition planet. We're a fucking moon base. We aren't subordinates waiting for orders. If our leaders had to be involved every time there was a disagreement, we would not get much trading done."

"You would all be in the brig." She frowned. "You said trading? Is that what you criminals call it these days?"

"Call what?"

"Oh, you know." She waved her hand in the air. "Human trafficking, selling drugs, selling weapons, selling *slaves.*" She crouched down. Moved closer to the corner. "Evil. You're all evil."

Uncaring of the risk, I crouched next to her and turned her to face me. "You speak of Cerberus and Siren Legions only. I am not evil, Ivy, and it is insulting after what we have been to each other to say that."

I gave her a pointed look, and she did, for a moment, look contrite. I continued on. "Astra does not deal in slaves. We sell weapons and armor, food, medical supplies. We steal from whomever we have to in order to make sure the people on the outer fringes survive. As I said, we are not part of the Coalition of Planets. We do not have ReGen wands in every room or ion blasters to fight off a Hive attack, not that they'd come here. We are, fortunately, irrelevant to them. So far. The people out here are forgotten and small. Our ruthless reputation helps keep us from their thoughts. We aren't chosen or included. We like it that way. We do whatever we need to do to survive."

She remained silent. I paused to regain control of my rage and asked the question I most needed an answer to. "Is that what you believe? That I am evil?"

There. For a moment, a fraction of a second the gentleness returned to her gaze, and she lifted her palm to cup my cheek. "No, Zenos. I know you are not evil. I'd say you're Robin Hood."

"Who?"

She shook her head. "No one."

I let it go, even though I had to wonder if this Robin Hood had been a previous male in her life. One who had also pleasured her into forgetting. One she'd fucked and left behind. Was he a fighter? A fellow rebel like her roaming the universe, bounty by bounty?

I gritted my teeth, then finally said, "Good." If I said anything more, I would make a fucking idiot of myself, worse than I already had over this female.

"Good," she repeated, lowering her hand, and my cheek went cold without her touch. "Let's go kick some ass."

9

Zenos

HER EXPRESSION CHANGED to fierce determination in the blink of an eye.

"What? No!" I barked a protest, but Ivy was on the move, swinging her hips like a siren as she sauntered across the street to the waiting crowd of enemies.

Fuck me. I dashed after her... toward sixteen fucking Cerberus males. If we survived this, she was going to get one hell of a spanking.

"Hi, boys."

Her smile was bright. The ignorant fools actually smiled back at her, pleased to see someone so attractive and appealing walking up to them—until I stepped into the light. Then their interest faded and several reached for their weapons. Ivy stopped just a few steps in front of the two largest males and spread her legs, her stance wide and bracing. She tilted her head in my direction and held up her hand toward me, palm out, in a silent order to stop moving. Shocked at the odd request, I did so.

"Don't worry about him, he's not so bad once you get to know him." I wasn't sure if she was taunting me or the Cerberus males.

Not so bad? What was this insane female doing? Was she trying to enrage *seventeen* males... me plus all of them? Apparently the Cerberus males had no idea how to deal with her either. What female sauntered up like this and had the audacity to confront them? With a smile and a swagger? She exuded sex, and they all were no doubt thinking dirty, filthy thoughts about what they wanted to do with her. *To* her.

No fucking way.

The two nearest her, both Prillon hybrids, paused their movements but kept their hands on their weapons. "What do you want, female?"

She shrugged. Holy fuck, she actually shrugged.

"Nothing, really. I'm just looking for an old friend of mine. Heard he likes to hang around here."

"Old friend, huh? You're not from Cerberus. You're not even from Rogue 5." A third hybrid—this one looked part Viken—stepped up to form a semicircle around Ivy, eyed every inch of her. I moved closer, but Ivy flashed her palm at me again.

Oh no, she didn't. She was worse than Astra, giving commands without saying a word. What fucking game was she playing here?

"Yes, an old friend," she repeated. She stood calm and quiet as the three males took their time answering her because they were *looking* her over. They would die.

"You are tall for a female," one stated. "Yet you do not look Atlan. What planet are you from?"

They knew she was an outsider. That probably made them lust for her more, to give a female from another planet a good Cerberus fucking.

"A little one," she replied vaguely. "Blue and white. A fair amount of green. But we don't like assholes much, so I don't recommend a visit."

Oh fuck. Not only did she walk right up to them, she poked at them with verbal jabs. She was doing it on purpose. This wasn't some naive female here, and that made me more pissed, more afraid.

The hybrid Prillon on her right growled at her insult, but the larger of the two held out his arm, holding his friend back. "I prefer to fuck females, not kill them, so state your business and get out of here or I'll quiet you and sample your pussy. When I'm done with you, I'll lock you in a cage on my ship and sell you to the highest bidder."

That would have scared anyone away. Not Ivy. *Fuck.*

That was going to happen over my dead body. This was just as I'd expected. She *knew* the Cerberus Legion was filled with a bunch of ruthless, lawless assholes. They didn't see her as as anything more than an object to use, to sell. And yet she was standing before them, *taunting* them.

Ivy's back stiffened at his remark, but not enough for the other males to notice. Only me. I knew her body. Knew the way she moved. Knew she was angry, but she had a plan, a reason for doing this. I just wished she'd clued me into it before now.

"I'm looking for someone, name of Gerian Eozara. Is he around?"

The hybrid Prillon who'd growled at her seconds ago now chuckled. "You have a death wish, female? Leave." He pointed toward the direction we'd come.

Ivy pulled a blade free from a hidden place on her body,

and my blood ran cold. He'd given her a chance to walk away, and she hadn't taken it. Did she really want to be raped and sold as a slave? If she had a death wish, there were simpler and less painful ways to die.

Fuck.

"I really, really need to talk to him," she said, pushing on with her agenda.

"Leave," the Viken hybrid repeated, this time looking up at me, assessing the situation. Giving me one last chance to drag the little rebel off before he carried through with his threats. "Leave here, both of you, before you spill blood."

Ivy continued to eye him, and I could hold still no longer. I moved forward, flanked her so no one could attack her from that direction. Starting a fight now was too dangerous. Sixteen to two. I had not been lying when I said I could kill them all, but I could not fight and watch over Ivy at the same time. If someone put a scratch on her, my focus would be gone. I'd be overtaken. We both would. We had to leave.

"Listen, I don't know you and you don't know me, but I'm not leaving this moon base without Gerian Eozara," she said. "Hand him over and I'll give you half the bounty on his head."

The two Prillon hybrids looked amused. "*You're* a bounty hunter? A small female from a small blue and white planet? How much is he worth these days? It must be quite a bit for you to dare come here like this."

Ivy shared a number that was staggering. The three males blinked. Slowly. But the hybrid Viken spoke for all of them, and I knew his words were true.

"We are Cerberus."

And that was that. Gerian Eozara was from the Cerberus Legion. He was one of them. The bounty could be worth ten times that amount, and no one from Cerberus Legion would even think of betraying one of their own. We were not like the other worlds. We were Rogue 5. Legions. We lived and died by the code of loyalty, and no one, not even the vile Cerberus or Siren Legion members broke that one, universal law. To break the code, to betray one's legion was certain death. It simply was not done. Ever.

They would not give up Gerian Eozara. We would get nothing further out of these males. We should leave now. Regroup... after I spanked Ivy's ass and set her straight once we were safely back in my quarters. Hell, setting her straight would mean tying her to my bed so she wouldn't pull a stunt like this again.

"And his little side business?" she prodded. "Dealing in Quell? You all know anything about that?"

The taller of the two Prillon hybrids answered this time. "It's the family business." He obviously felt no shame in what was peddled. Addiction and death.

Ivy paused and nodded, seemed to understand that these males were not going to lead her to her quarry, or at least I assumed she did until she grinned. "I was hoping you would say that."

I had seen her naked, coming all over my cock. I had seen her argue with Astra and hold a small boy in her lap. But I had never seen her fight and I didn't want to.

Fuck, those were fighting words. I recognized them and her tall stance. The tension in her muscles, the gleam in her eye.

"Ivy, no," I warned.

Other members of Cerberus Legion poured out of the building in a flood to see what was occurring. Their numbers doubled, then tripled. They circled around us.

And Ivy, my beautiful Ivy didn't cower, didn't even blink. She fucking smiled. "Now this is more like it."

She wasn't panicking, but I was. I'd lost count of the number of Cerberus who now surrounded us.

"Ivy, we are leaving. *Now*." I put every ounce of dominance in my voice. It was a command, nothing less. My fangs were fully extended, and every instinct I had raged at me to get both of us the fuck out of here. There were too many of them now. I couldn't protect her against this many, not alone. We were going to leave or die. I was in charge here, assigned to protect her. She'd given me her word to obey if her life was in danger.

And... she wasn't listening. She wasn't *obeying*.

She was *smiling*.

What. The. Fuck?

We were riding the edge between life and death. We were deep in Cerberus Legion. We had no legion armband on. No one from Astra knew where we were. No one was coming to help us. Not here. We were in danger, and I expected to be obeyed.

Blade swirling in her palm, she glanced over her shoulder at me and grinned, completely ignoring the two Prillon hybrids looming over her like she was carrion.

"Not yet, baby," she said to me as if placating a small child. She looked amused, almost *eager* to fight. She appeared relaxed, but I sensed the anticipation, the tension in her body ready to be unleashed. "This will just take a few minutes."

A few minutes? We'd be dead in a few minutes.

My breath caught in my throat, half panic, half paralyzed by the gleam of eagerness in her gaze—and more. She'd called me *baby*. What did that—

I blinked and she'd moved, her blade slicing through the

two Prillon hybrids like they were made of air. I knew differently, knew what it took to slice through the protective band of armor at the base of their throats, their large bodies. Skin, tendon, bone.

Ivy shouldn't have been able to...

The hybrid Viken fell next, his neck twisted at an odd angle as Ivy leaped over his head—way over his head—and landed in the center of a group of Cerberus Enforcers at least ten paces closer to the building. Holy fuck, she had to be an Everian Hunter to move like that.

The others, at first stunned at what she'd done, now swarmed her like insects. The attack, her explosion of movement had lasted just a second or two.

My mind tried to process, to understand what I was seeing. *What Ivy was doing.* All by herself.

It was impossible. This was not happening. My eyes weren't working properly.

She disappeared from view, buried beneath the pile of attackers, and the possessive rage within me exploded. I'd vowed to keep her safe, and I was failing. Finally I moved. I attacked, flinging bodies, uncaring of the path of destruction I left in my wake. If they blocked my path to Ivy, they died. I had to reach her. To save her.

"No!"

My bellow of rage seemed to snap a few of the peripheral bystanders to their senses. A few turned and ran because this wasn't just a female who'd ended up in the wrong place at the wrong time. This wasn't fun and games for them anymore. If they hadn't fled, they'd have taken their last breaths. The ones who bolted were the smart ones. They didn't have a death wish. Not for themselves.

The others I tore to pieces with my bare hands. Two. Five. Ten. Ion blaster fire bounced off my new armor exactly as the smuggler had promised Astra it would when we'd bought it. I felt the cut of several blades, but they were nothing. Last-ditch efforts to protect themselves. Annoyances that preceded the attackers' deaths.

I plowed through the Cerberus fighters, but when I reached the place Ivy had disappeared, I found nothing but a pile of dead and dying, none of them Ivy. My female was nowhere to be seen.

"Ivy!"

My bellow echoed up and down the street, and I realized how quiet things had become. Dead bodies were strewn about my feet, the others having either run away to wait for reinforcements or taken refuge inside. They'd all given up. Fled.

But where the fuck was my female?

My head whipped around at the sound of ion blasts from inside the canteen. Shouting. Screams.

Oh, shit. She went *inside*?

Enraged—at Ivy and everyone who was shooting at her —I stalked to the door to open it, my blood-slicked hand wrapped around the handle. Glass shattered and I jumped back. A body flew through the air to hit the street with a loud groan.

Not Ivy, but a hulking hybrid Atlan in fucking beast mode. He had to be close to my height, my size. He'd been so enraged his beast had taken over, yet he'd been tossed out a window as if he were a piece of food scrap given to a pet.

Turning, I watched in awe as Ivy leaped through the open section of window—she'd completely destroyed the scene displaying a peaceful Atlan landscape—to crouch on the ground next to a pile of bodies. Scanned the group for threats. No, she wasn't part Everian. She was something else entirely, something I'd never seen before.

A female I recognized as one of Cerberus's top Enforcers lay at the edge. Jillela. The female was a skilled and ruthless fighter. Cruel and brutal, yet she, too, lay broken among her legion members. Alive but unable to fight.

"Cerberus will hunt you down," Jillela warned, her voice tinged with pain, her breathing ragged. "You will die for this."

Her threat made my blood boil, and I ached to rip her body in half for daring to threaten Ivy.

Ivy stood, walked over to her. Loomed. "You tell Cerberus that I'm coming back, and I'll keep coming back, keep killing you drug-running fucks until he gives me what I want." Blood covered Ivy's hands, her blade and uniform, but she wasn't even breathing hard. Didn't even have sweat on her brow after killing or injuring at least thirty Cerberus. What. The. Fuck?

"And what is that, you Hived-Up piece of shit?" Jillela glared, wincing as she tried to move. Ivy put a booted foot on the female's shoulder and pushed her back down.

I froze as if stunned by a blaster. What had Jillela said? *Hived-Up?*

No.

Please, by the gods, no. Was *that* what her scar had been from? Was that the reason she'd been so confused by little Scylla's attentions? She'd intentionally had Hive integrations imbedded in her body?

"Gerian Eozara. I get Gerian, I'm gone. Out of your hair." Ivy set her foot down on the ground, and the fact that the hardest female in Cerberus didn't dare move shocked me almost as much as her words had.

Hived-Up? My Ivy? That was impossible. No one but the foulest of the foul willingly went to the black markets run by the outlying worlds and bought Hive tech. *Paid* to have their body mutilated. Contaminated. Paid hack scientists to implant experimental and unpredictable *enhancements* into their bodies to make them stronger, better, faster. Ruthless and lethal and able to... *to kill a large swath of Cerberus Legion without even breaking a sweat.* It was considered offensive, vile, even on Rogue 5, and compared to the Coalition Fleet, our standards were exceptionally low.

Yet Ivy had done the impossible. I'd seen it firsthand, was witnessing the aftermath right now. I had all the proof I needed to believe it, even if I didn't want to.

"I don't know that name." Jillela lied to the bounty hunter staring down at her, and I held my breath, waiting to see if Ivy would allow her to live for the insult.

Ivy dropped on top of the woman faster than I could blink, her blade pressed to the female's throat. "Well then, I guess I should just kill you and find a better messenger."

I'd never seen Jillela afraid before. Never. Not even with the largest of foes. She was a formidable and ruthless opponent, but with Ivy she was petrified. "No. No need. I... I will deliver your message."

Jillela's fearful eyes roamed the destruction, the dead. I saw the wheels turning in her mind, the counting as she assessed the threat, the truth of Ivy's words. The extent of what one female could do in her quest to find Gerian Eozara.

Cerberus was not a small force, there were several hundred members they could send after Ivy. But the human female had just killed at least a dozen of the worst of Cerberus and injured a dozen or so more, without elevating her heart rate. I'd killed as well, but we were not banded with legion colors. This wasn't a legion versus legion fight. It was personal, the work of a female who was out for vengeance, and those in the Cerberus Legion who got in her way were either injured and broken, like Jillela, or dead.

This destruction was on them. That was our code. Even so, I had no doubt Cerberus would triple his guard and every single one of them on patrol would be out for blood. For Ivy. For the Hived-Up human ex-Coalition fighter.

We wouldn't get this deep into Cerberus territory again. At least not without killing a few of them along the way. But looking at Ivy, I didn't think that would stop her.

She hadn't gotten her bounty, but she'd certainly gotten the message out that she was after him... and would get him. At any price.

"Thank you," Ivy said to Jillela as if they were having dinner together like close friends. "You have until this time tomorrow, or I'll be back."

Yeah, not friends.

"And how am I supposed to find you?" Jillela wondered. "You aren't one of us. You are not Rogue 5."

If anyone like Ivy had grown up on Rogue 5, she'd be infamous regardless of legion. Everyone would know of her abilities, just like Jillela knew she was not from here.

"No, I'm not. I'm a bounty hunter." Ivy rose and turned, pointed a bloody finger at me. "You know who he is, don't you?"

The female lifted her head from the ground and looked at me. Our gazes locked. "Zenos."

"Jillela." I returned her greeting as a golden angel with ice-cold blue eyes stood above her like death incarnate.

"Find Zenos, you find me." Ivy clapped her hands together. "Excellent. That's now settled. We'll be on our way."

Ivy sauntered toward me, her hips swinging, every curve and muscle under her control, leaving Jillela behind.

Now that the panic for her safety had bled away like the lifeblood of the Cerberus on the ground before us, I could see Ivy for what she really was. She was contained violence. Lovely death. Primal. Vicious. Protective. She was here to avenge her Coalition unit, her friends who had died. They weren't her family, but they meant something to her, as the other members of Astra Legion did to me. Not related by blood but by circumstance, by war. She'd gone into Cerberus territory armed with only a blade, blasters and the skill of her body to avenge her friends. To seek the one responsible.

I'd known all that, she'd told me. Us. Astra. Barek, the others. But I hadn't understood the extent of it, how much it drove her. How far she'd go to achieve her goal.

Had she gotten herself Hived-Up for this purpose? To help her in avenging them? Fuck, if that was true, she'd gone to unbelievable lengths to do so. She hadn't gotten the integrations for selfish reasons. The opposite. She'd endured pain, even the sneer and hatred of others, for her unit. Entering Cerberus Legion was *nothing*. This fight? It had been *nothing* to her.

She would not stop until her loved ones were avenged. The look I'd seen on her face when little Nero had climbed into her lap, the panic, the confusion, must have been because she didn't understand love and connection that wasn't forged by battle. She had everything within her to be the perfect mate, the perfect mother, she just didn't realize it.

She knew nothing but revenge. For fighting. For justice. She'd turned herself into something she detested in order to accomplish the only thing on her mind. Her sole focus.

Once this need for justice was complete, she would learn the truth of herself. I would show her she was more than just a machine out for vengeance. She would be protective of our children. Our legion. Our home.

But those were dangerous thoughts. She'd told me she did not want a mate, and what she'd just done, how she'd single-handedly destroyed a group of Cerberus, was indication enough that her focus wasn't on those types of pursuits. Settling down, creating a home and a life with someone else? Creating children and the nesting and preparation that came with that? No, what female killed and maimed while eager to carry a child in her womb? Even if she were pining for an infant of her own, my bite was most likely lethal and she would not get a child from me. We could fuck, but I could never claim her. I could not risk her life. She could have died here on the streets, yet I was most fearful of killing her myself.

My soul cried for her, for what she was. Inside. She was a monster like me. A powerful, loyal, merciless monster. The most beautiful thing I'd ever fucking seen.

Ivy touched my shoulder as she walked past. "Come on, Zenos. She knows where to find me, and I really need a shower." She turned around but continued to walk backward. "And that fuck you promised. Something about licking my clit?"

10

Ivy, Astra Legion, Zenos's Private Quarters

I SHOOK. Hot water poured over me, but the heat did nothing to soothe my frayed nerves. The adrenaline was bleeding away, leaving me edgy and twitchy.

I'd killed before, in battle, on missions, but never with such cold rage. Surrounded by those guys from Cerberus, I'd had a blood lust so intense I'd been hyper-focused, almost desperate for destruction. And I'd caused it. They might not be the ones directly involved with poisoning my unit with Quell, but they condoned it. Allowed it to happen. They were accomplices, the ones responsible for my units' deaths, my suffering, the scars I carried like brands of shame.

And God help me, I'd seen Zenos's face when the female, Jillela, had named me a monster. *Hived-Up.*

I hated that fucking term. To me, one who'd spent years fighting the Hive, it was a pejorative, as if getting the nanotech and integrations by choice was a good thing. Fuck no. The term was insulting, as if I were a traitor to my own people. When I'd had it done, it was true, it felt like I was betraying my unit all over again, as if I were killing each one of their souls for the sake of my own. I'd done it for *them*.

And I didn't get Hived-Up. I'd *lived*. I was surviving, that was all. Sure, a quick fuck made me forget for a short time, but that was all. I didn't forget. I couldn't. *Everything* I did was for them. Revenge. Retribution. Justice. Even the integrations.

It was *all* for them.

The truth should not hurt so badly, yet it did. I'd done what I had to do to survive on that backward outpost after my unit went down. My will to live had overcome every other objection. I had taken what was offered to be stronger, better, faster and hid the shame. Until today. Until Zenos saw the truth with his own eyes, heard it from Jillela. He'd looked at me like I was less than human. Less than a Rogue hybrid. Less than the dirt beneath his boot.

I was. Yet I was more. I'd proved it with the destruction I'd left strewn behind me in Cerberus dead. I was faster than an Everian, stronger than an Atlan beast. More cunning than a Prillon commander.

"Damn it." I punched the wall of the shower, leaving a dent in the thick metallic surface.

"Save your rage for battle, female." Zenos's deep voice stopped me cold, and I turned my head, looked over my shoulder at him. He was clean. Naked. Looking me over through the clear wall of the shower tube, his gaze lingered where the small cuts from Cerberus blades stung in the water. I purposely left my back exposed to him. He'd seen me naked before, but not like this. The stupid armor somehow highlighted scars, what I'd done. Little Scylla had pointed it out to me, how she'd seen my long scar even through my shirt. Zenos had known before that the markings on my body existed, from the first time we met on Zenith.

Now he knew *why*. Knew what the scars meant. He'd called me brave. Honorable. I was contaminated with Hive technology. Dirty. Vile.

I was even more rogue than Zenos. I was more rogue than the evil of Cerberus or Siren. Those legions might have zero morals or ethics and sell humans for coin, but I was the worst enemy of all: Hive.

"What do you want, Zenos?" I couldn't face him. Not like this. Naked. Exposed. Real. What had I thought? I'd go all wild with my new integrations and he'd never learn the truth? That I wouldn't care if he learned the truth?

Yeah, that was what I'd thought. I hadn't given a shit what anyone thought of me until now. Until him.

Turning my face away, I rested my forehead against the cool wall and sighed. "Just leave me alone. I'll be gone soon enough. You won't have to protect me from myself any longer."

Cool air was the only indication that the door had opened. Hands gripped my waist and lifted me, pressed my chest to the cool wall. Held me securely. I rested my cheek against the hard surface. "That is not acceptable, female."

I spread my arms like I would if doing a push-up and pressed back. Hard. Using every ounce of my artificial strength, showing him exactly who and what I was. Reminding him since he'd clearly forgotten, even though it had been only a short time ago I'd left a path of destruction in my wake. "Let me go," I snapped.

"No." His hands rested over mine, his hot breath burning the back of my wet neck. "I have never seen a female more beautiful. You are a goddess of death. A gorgeous, vengeful goddess." His hard cock pressed to my lower back, and I shuddered with lust.

He was hard for me? Impossible. I was a freak.

"What are you doing?" I pushed again. Harder. But he still didn't budge. He was strong. So damn strong. Why was he being nice? He knew the truth now, that I was part Hive, part enemy. That I'd gone to extremes to live and used that to my advantage, to rip through a group of Cerberus.

His lips traced the outline of my ear, licked away the water on my skin. "Do you want me to stop, Ivy? Truly? Or do you want me to fuck you raw?"

Oh God. My pussy went into spasm, tightening, pulsing. Aching for what was pressed to my back. I needed it. I needed him to help me forget, to make me feel good for even a little while. To turn this hatred I had at myself into something better.

"Fuck me."

There was no more talking. I didn't want the truth. I didn't want to hear it, to know what he thought of me now. With a groan he lifted me high enough to position his cock at my entrance and thrust deep. Hard. Fast.

I cried out at the penetration. The feel of being stretched open, taken completely.

I had nowhere to go, nowhere to run. I was trapped between a hard wall and a hard body, his cock filling me completely. There was no escape as he took me. He wasn't gentle, but I didn't want that. I wanted the rough jerks of his hips, the deep strokes, the slap of flesh on flesh. He consumed me. Filled me. Made me forget.

His fangs grazed my shoulder, and I cried out, my core clamping down on his cock like a fist from wanting them. Yes. God yes. I wanted him to fucking bite me. Claim me. He knew the truth now. Knew everything. Knew what I was, what I would always be. If he bit me now, claimed me, *wanted me,* I would stay. Fight beside him. Defend his people and his legion. Protect little Scylla and Nero.

All he had to do was one thing. Turn his head, sink his fangs deep.

Bite me.

"Come now," he urged, his thrusts unrelenting. "Come all over my cock, Ivy. Give me what I want."

He thrust deeper. Shifted his angle. Groaned. I moaned as he pushed me to the brink.

"Come. Say my name. Fucking say it," he snapped.

"Bite me," I begged. I couldn't help myself. I wanted what I wanted. Him. All of him. His cock. His body. His heart. His mating mark. His bite.

His venom.

"Do it," I taunted. "Bite me."

I was giving myself to him with those words. I'd give up everything, my need for vengeance, my need to roam, to drift through the galaxy alone. One little thing and I'd become his, *give* myself to him.

His fangs scratched the surface of my skin just enough to hurt, and I exploded, his name torn from my throat as I obeyed his command to come, my pussy milking his cock. Colors danced behind my eyes, my scream echoed off the thin walls of the bathing tube.

Bite me.

He was going to do it. Sink his fangs deep. Give me his essence. Make me his.

Fuck yes. I tried to gain purchase on the wall, but my fingers slipped. There was no purchase, no way to hang on to my control with him. Like my hold, I was willing to slip away. For him. Only him.

The thought made me come again, one orgasm running into another as he fucked me through it, fast and wild, pushing me higher.

With a groan he tore his lips from my flesh as his cock pulsed inside me. His cum filled me, scorching hot. Aftershocks made me tremble for long minutes as he held me pinned to the wall, our hands joined, fingers entwined. I had never felt like I was not myself before. Not me. The other half of *him*. Half of *us*.

So why were tears streaking my cheeks?

He'd given me pleasure but nothing else. *Bite me.* He hadn't. He wouldn't. Since he knew the truth of what I really was, of course he wouldn't. Who'd want to be mated to me? Not Zenos.

I'd begged. *Begged.* And he had refused. Denied me. Again.

Swallowing hard, I willed the tears to stop before he could see them, thankful we were in the shower tube, the water raining upon us hiding them.

He wasn't going to claim me. Ever. I had to make peace with that fact. I was Hived-Up. Contaminated. Less. Oh, he'd fuck me and help me work off the post-fight rush of adrenaline. He'd make me feel good, but now, when I'd hoped he'd make me forget all the bad in my life, it would only make me remember the one thing I could never have.

Him. I would never be his completely. I'd never be whole.

I should have heeded his original warning in the canteen. I didn't belong here on Rogue 5, I didn't belong dragging him to an empty room on Zenith and seducing him. I should have looked away from the gorgeous hybrid Forsian in the bar. I should have been stronger. It was too damn late now. I was in love with the big jerk, and he would fuck me—my aching, well-used pussy could confirm that—but not claim me.

Lesson learned. Message received. I wouldn't ask again.

I was done.

When my body relaxed in his arms, he pulled free, rinsed us both off and carried me to his bed. The endorphins from the battle and from the sex faded, and exhaustion dragged me under as his fingertips traced the nicks and scars on my arms. My neck. He rolled so that I lay sprawled on top of him, a blanket creating a cocoon of warmth and safety over us. I didn't say anything. There were no words left.

I was with him, in his arms, but we were separate, entities unto ourselves.

This was temporary, along with everything else in my life.

This wasn't reality, this was another world. Another place. In this moment I was somewhere I didn't have to worry about someone killing me or hunting me or demanding that I board a transport with my ReCon unit and charge into enemy territory. I didn't have to think, worry. But I couldn't help but feel. Not just his heated skin, but the hard planes of muscle beneath. The beat of his heart. Everything that was touching me but would never be mine.

His hand moved gently up and down my back, lingered on the marks I knew created a patchwork of history and pain. That were made by the enemy. That made *me* the enemy, in a way. That made me more rogue than he could deal with. He caressed me like I was a fragile kitten, and my body purred. It was impossible to resist, and because of it I was doomed. I sank into his heat, taking what I could get while I could get it, and I slept.

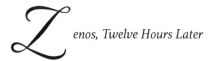

enos, Twelve Hours Later

"ARE YOU WELL?" I asked.

"I'm fine." Ivy walked beside me, her silence a mystery I had been unable to unravel since she'd woken in my arms. I had held her for long hours and stared at the ceiling as she slept, waited for the knock I knew would come to my door.

Jillela would deliver Ivy's message, I had no doubt. I'd seen the fear in Jillela's eyes, knew she was more afraid of Ivy than anything before. Perhaps she was even more afraid of her than Cerberus himself.

Astra would hear of what had happened, of the dead we'd left behind. I was not worried that my leader would chastise us. Ivy was a weapon of mass destruction that currently belonged to her. She would be pleased.

Cerberus alone was responsible for anything that went on in his territory, even a female destroyer. I had been acting alone. As a rebel. As a bounty hunter in league with Ivy. It may not have been known Gerian Eozara had a large bounty on his head before, but after last night, after what Ivy had done all on her own, everyone on the moon base, regardless of legion, now knew. Gerian Eozara was a wanted man.

Ivy would not be the last to come looking for him. Fuck that. Once word spread, there would be unmarked members of every legion taking their shot.

The bounty was exceptional. That kind of money bought ships—and not the decades-old, battle-scarred Coalition Fleet ships that had seen better days. One could purchase a new ship, with the newest and deadliest weapons. Cloaking technology. Speed. The kind of ship that could create a mini empire on Rogue 5. Gerian's days were numbered. And while Cerberus might not hand him over to an enemy, their legion would not be excited about keeping him around either. His own people would want him dead for financial gain.

Soon Gerian would be one of two things—dead or long gone, assigned to a job somewhere else so the flow of bounty hunters seeking a big payday would stop. The last thing Cerberus wanted was strangers snooping around his legion causing trouble. Especially strangers like Ivy.

Ivy was the first, but she wouldn't be the last, and she'd made one hell of a mess.

Cerberus was a mean fucking bastard. He was not stupid. He would not welcome more attention, more bounty hunters or challenges from the others on Rogue 5 eager to collect on the bounty. Cerberus would act, and soon. *Very soon.*

We walked to the meeting hall, escorted by Barek. He walked in front of us, Ivy in the middle, and I watched her back. It was instinct, and I didn't ever want to be anywhere else. After the night before and what she'd done, I had to wonder if she needed me. She was so fucking self-sufficient, so brave and strong. She could handle anything. Yet I wasn't going anywhere.

"What's going on, Barek?" she asked.

He glanced over his shoulder at her, saying nothing, his rumble of displeasure did not improve my mood. Not with Ivy refusing to talk to me. I had believed I understood the meaning of her word *fine,* but she was not acting in accordance with the definition in my mind. Perhaps I needed to have my NPU checked to make sure the translation function worked well with Earth languages.

Physically she was fine. I'd run my hands over every inch of her as we'd fucked in the shower tube and later in bed. But females were complicated creatures. A few orgasms wouldn't solve their problems. They didn't have balls to empty, to lull the mind and sate the body.

They were complex, and Ivy was no exception.

Ivy appeared to be as impatient as I for an answer. "Did Cerberus send word?" she asked, pushing him.

"You two made a fucking mess, you know that?" Barek snapped, shaking his head. Ah, word *had* spread.

Ivy shrugged as if Barek's words meant nothing. I could not hold my tongue.

"We were not wearing Astra's colors." As if that made the destruction she'd caused any better.

"That is why you are not dead." Barek led us down a small corridor to a secured meeting area I'd seen many times before. Astra used the room for discussions with sensitive clients or high-ranking members of the other legions when discretion was required. The room held no more than ten, and the walls were insulated and scanned daily. No one would overhear. No sound spilled through the walls, and there were several tunnels into and out of the meeting space. Anyone brought inside was blindfolded and searched prior to entry so they would not attempt to find their way back again.

I'd once led a Siren messenger up and down the same hallways for over an hour to make sure he was well and truly lost prior to a meeting.

Some died within the walls, their screams did not escape. They entered alive, exited dead and were never seen or heard of again. I didn't think we were walking to our deaths, but it was possible Astra wanted to rid her legion of Ivy. And myself, because I would die first.

The door slid open, and we followed Barek into the room to find Astra already seated at one end of a long table, Rhord and Nev behind her.

I paused in the doorway, took in the rest of the inhabitants.

Sitting at the other end of the table was Cerberus himself, Jillela standing behind him with another member of the legion a few paces back. They all seemed healthy and whole, meaning they'd either spent the time since we'd seen them last in a ReGen pod or had made liberal use of a wand. And at his feet? A male I assumed was Gerian Eozara, handcuffed and on his knees. Bloodied, possibly stunned into submission.

A gift. The offering Ivy had been waiting for.

I'd assumed things would happen fast, but this was surely a record. Cerberus wanted this over.

Barek walked to Astra's side and nodded at Rhord to stand guard at the door. Ivy took two steps into the room, glanced at her quarry and froze.

She'd spent months for this moment, to get the one responsible for her unit's deaths. Now he was here, on his knees, restrained. Cerberus may have delivered him, but she'd done it.

But it wasn't over. Not yet.

Cerberus looked Ivy over, shock clearly evident in his wide eyes as he took in the small female who had single-handedly killed so many of his best fighters. No doubt the stories he'd heard had been epic. "So you are the bounty hunter I've been hearing so much about."

"I am." Ivy answered him but looked at Jillela. The female wasn't still marked by her time with Ivy and her trip through the glass window, but I saw fear there. Trepidation. She looked like she'd been kicked by more than just Ivy's boot. She was no longer the fearless fighter I knew. "Jillela."

"Ivy."

That was quite civilized, but I didn't expect Ivy to leap across the table and beat Jillela up. There weren't rules, but there were *rules*. Ivy seemed to know how to behave in a setting like this. In this moment when everything she'd been working toward was kneeling before her. She was too smart to blow it now.

Cerberus cleared his throat. "I don't normally respond to demands like yours, bounty hunter, but to be honest I was fascinated and had to meet you." "Should I be flattered?" Ivy asked, clearly not.

"Yes."

That was a surprise. I doubted Cerberus ever dealt out praise, even to his own.

Cerberus rose and I stepped between him and my female. He was not a Forsian hybrid, but he was large. Fast. More Hyperion than male, or so I'd heard. He was a brutal and efficient killer, and I did not want him anywhere near Ivy. Fuck that, I didn't want them in the same room. Yet here we were.

Ivy ignored his comment and moved around me so she could see Cerberus once more. I wanted to growl at her but held my tongue. Barely, and only because I knew now how ruthless she was. If anyone could match him in a fight, it was her. That didn't mean I wanted it to occur.

"Did you bring me a gift?" she asked, staring down at the prisoner.

"I did." Cerberus flicked his gaze at Gerian Eozara as if he were a pest.

At last Astra joined the conversation. "What do you want in return for this gift, Cerberus?"

Cerberus looked at my leader. "From you? Nothing. From her?" He moved closer to Ivy and I growled this time, but Cerberus raised his hands, palms out, and stopped moving. "Easy, Zenos. I came to offer Ivy a deal, nothing more."

Cerberus didn't *deal* with anyone.

"Then state your business and get out of my territory." That was Astra, and she was losing patience with Cerberus and his games.

"I want the name of your maker, Ivy. That is all. I want to know who worked on your body. Who made you?"

He spoke as if Ivy weren't real, as if she were a cyborg, a fully integrated Hive machine. She was human. She was flesh and bone. She had emotion. Feelings. Regrets. Hive tech, definitely, but that didn't define her.

Cerberus didn't see her that way. He saw power. Strength beyond normal abilities. A weapon.

Ivy crossed her arms over her chest, a calculating look in her eyes. "To be clear, if I tell you where I got my integrations and who did them, you'll hand over Gerian and walk away?"

He nodded in agreement, which was stunning in itself.

"Yes." There was an almost fanatical fervor in his eyes. He wanted to be what she was. Stronger. Faster. Hive. Integrated.

Contaminated. And he'd just hand over one of his own in trade. A life for a name.

Fuck, Ivy wasn't contaminated. She was perfect.

"The Coalition will hunt you if they discover the truth," she warned.

"Clearly they have yet to learn the truth about you." Cerberus shrugged. "Besides, they hunt me already. I am not afraid of the Coalition."

That was true. No legion leader was afraid of the Coalition. None of us on Rogue 5 were. Ivy turned to Astra. "Is there any reason you would not wish me to reveal this information to him?"

Astra's eyes widened in surprise, but it was clear she was pleased that Ivy had asked. Had deferred to her in this. In her own way Ivy was already protecting us. Serving Astra. Her secret was a bargaining piece, and she was giving it to Astra to use, not to hoard for herself.

"No. Tell him if you wish." Astra's gaze narrowed, and she tilted her head in an angle meant to mock the other leader. "Hive tech will not be enough to help him rule Rogue 5."

Cerberus laughed, but there was no humor in the sound. "I am not so ambitious, Astra."

"Liar." The word slipped from me before I thought to sensor it, but I did not care whether I insulted the evil male before me. Everyone looked to me but remained silent. Cerberus could have struck out for the insolence, but what I spoke was the truth and he knew it. He had a bargaining piece on his knees, but he was not the one in control. Ivy was.

Ivy looked from Astra, who nodded, to Barek, who stood without expression, to me. Her gaze locked with mine. Lingered. She wanted something from me, but I could not fathom what that might be. When she released me from her gaze to face Cerberus again, I nearly growled aloud in frustration.

Females. I did not understand them. I protected her. I held her. I made her scream with pleasure and cared for her as she slept. I had fought beside her and killed for her. I *let* her run wild among the deadliest members of Cerberus Legion. And yet in that moment, I knew that somehow I had failed her.

"His name is Levenagen. You'll find him at a trading outpost on a planet called Xerima."

Cerberus grinned, clearly pleased with himself. He'd gotten what he wanted at no expense to him. Gerian Eozara meant nothing more to him than a mere pawn to trade.

"I have heard of this place, the people there are as wild as pure Hyperions."

"So I've heard," Ivy said.

"The trade is complete." Cerberus tipped his chin to the prisoner. "He is yours."

She looked down at Gerian, where he remained on his knees, looking like a beaten animal. "Astra, may I ask a favor?"

"Another?"

Ivy grinned. "Yes. Can you please have that piece of shit dragged to some kind of holding cell while I make transport arrangements? I have a bounty to collect."

"Of course." Astra rose. "Rhord. Nev. See our guests to the exit."

Guests was used so courteously yet meant anything but.

While a deal had been made, peacefully, Cerberus was still the enemy.

"Yes, Astra." Nev stepped forward, Rhord on his heels, but Cerberus still stared at my female. He wanted her. Sexually, I had no doubt, which made me want to rip his head off, but she also intrigued him. She was the most ruthless tool he knew. She was alive, breathing... here. He wanted her as his own.

Over my fucking dead body. "You need to leave." I glared at the male, eager for an excuse to hurt him. Kill him.

Cerberus looked my way, then to Ivy. "Turning in Gerian will not change a thing, Lieutenant Ivy Birkeland of Earth." Cerberus lifted his chin to signal Jillela, and she moved toward the exit, to where Nev and Rhord stood waiting to take them back through the tunnels.

Ivy's back went ramrod straight. "It will stop him from selling more Quell."

Cerberus laughed. The bastard laughed in Ivy's face. "I have dozens more where he came from. This changes nothing. You came all the way out here to stop the flow of Quell?" His laughter turned mocking. "You are a fool after all. So disappointing. I had high hopes for you, Ivy. I even entertained the idea of recruiting you, my dear. You are an excellent killer."

I hated his words, the taunt behind them, but I remained silent. He was leaving, and that was what I wanted more than anything.

Cerberus followed Jillela out of the room. The moment the door slid closed behind him, Astra came around the table. Barek grabbed Gerian and pulled the prisoner to his feet as my leader approached Ivy. "You have what you came for, Ivy. You kept your end of the bargain, and I have kept mine."

Ivy bowed in respect. "Agreed. Thank you."

Astra nodded. "Good. Now, you have twenty-four hours to get out of my territory. If you aren't mine, you can't stay. Understand?"

"Yes. I'll be gone long before that. I'll be out of here in twelve."

"Excellent." Astra turned to Gerian, eyed him like he was a scum. "Learned your lesson too late, didn't you?"

"What lesson is that?" he snarled. In Barek's tight hold, that was all he could do. "That Cerberus is a backstabbing bastard?"

Astra laughed. "No. Everyone knows that. If you didn't, you're more a fool than I thought." Her gaze flitted to Ivy, then back to Gerian. "You never turn your back on a powerful woman, especially after you kill her family."

"I didn't—"

"Shut up and move." Barek shoved Gerian forward, the smaller male stumbling through the doorway. Astra followed. The door slid closed, and I was alone with Ivy.

She paced like a caged tiger in the small space. "He's right. Cerberus was right. I killed all those people last night for nothing."

"They were Cerberus." That was all the justification I, or anyone on Rogue 5, needed for what had happened. For the carnage she'd caused.

She eyed me. "Are you telling me that Cerberus Legion doesn't have children? Innocents?"

"Of course they do, but none of them were at the fight. They were home, asleep. Their mothers safe taking care of their children. We killed no innocents, Ivy. Do not torture yourself with guilt."

She exhaled harshly. "But I failed."

"You caught Gerian. You will receive your reward. You will be wealthy, Ivy. And you have avenged your loved ones."

"Have I?" She shook her head, almost as if defeated. As if she realized that even though she'd captured Gerian Eozara, it wouldn't bring her teammates back. "I don't think so. He's right. The Quell will keep coming. I need to take it out at the source. I need to kill Cerberus and blow up the lab."

What? Surely I was hearing things. Kill Cerberus? Was she fucking insane?

"Ivy, no. Our spies reported that their labs are deep within Cerberus Legion's territory here. We would never make it alive." I moved closer, reached for her shoulder. I wanted nothing more than to pull her into my arms, comfort her, convince her to stay. "You should take Gerian and collect your bounty. Live in peace. That is what your friends would want for you."

"It's too late for that." Her eyelids dropped, and her body seemed to lose all its energy. "No. I have twelve hours. I'm going to take him out, him and his lab." She jerked away from my touch and stepped back, her blue eyes lifting to mine. "If I don't come back, take Gerian to Zenith and ask a Coalition officer there to connect you with Elite Hunter Sabir. He works with the Intelligence Core. He'll tell you what you need to do to collect the bounty."

This wasn't what I expected. She wasn't done? Gerian wasn't enough? When would it end? Would destroying the lab truly finish it? They'd build another, but I wasn't going to tell her that. Instead I reminded her, "He is worth a small fortune, Ivy. You should have the reward."

"It's not about the fucking money. Don't you get that yet?" She paced, tugged at her braid. "It was never about the money."

I straightened my spine. "You will not go back to Cerberus Legion. I forbid it."

Her blue eyes were cold once more. Ice fucking cold. "I gave you my word I would not go anywhere without informing you. That I wouldn't go anywhere that put me in danger. You saw me last night, I was never in danger. And that was only while you were responsible for me. That is no longer the case. I'm truly rogue now. I'm informing you anyway, as a courtesy. I'm going. If I don't come back, take Gerian in. Collect the reward. If you don't want it, give it to Scylla and Nero's parents."

"I forbid it." Stepping forward, I backed her into the wall, blocking her exit. "You will not go back there. I will tie you to my bed, Lieutenant. I will strip you naked and fuck you so hard you won't remember how to get to Cerberus."

She glared, her chest heaving. Nipples hard. I could smell her arousal. Her welcoming heat. "Yeah? And then what?"

I frowned. "I do not understand."

She looked away. "That's what I thought." She shoved her way past me, and I let her go, unsure of what to do next. Unsure of what she meant.

I followed her into the corridor, unwilling to let her out of my sight. She was volatile. Dangerous. And I knew she meant what she'd said. Yet I could not allow her to risk her life by returning to Cerberus Legion.

She moved like a shadow, making no sound as we worked our way back toward my quarters. When we arrived, she stripped off the uniform Astra had given her and put her own Coalition uniform back on. I did nothing but watch. I was at a loss, confused by her new drive. By her words. Something had shifted between us, but I didn't know what it was. When she rose to leave, I stood as well, blocking the door. "I cannot allow this, Ivy. I'm sorry."

Her blue eyes met mine. Held. "So am I."

She lifted her hand to reveal an ion blaster. Too late I realized exactly how far she would go to destroy her enemies. The blast hit me square in the chest and threw my body back against the wall. I fell, snarling as I fought to rise, but the weapon had been set to stun and it had worked. I couldn't move.

"I am going to spank your ass until you beg my forgiveness, female," I warned, struggling against the stun to get up. It was impossible. "Then I'm going to make you ride my cock until you scream."

It seemed that wasn't much of a threat because she fired again and I slid to the ground, a red haze of burning agony stealing my consciousness as she bent over me. The stun setting had been high.

I fought to stay with her, to protect her. I could not pass out, could not fall. She would leave. She would go to Cerberus Legion alone. She would be in danger.

She leaned close and kissed me, gently, on the cheek. "You would spank me and make me scream, but you wouldn't bite me, would you, Zenos?"

I growled, still fighting. Barely. "Cannot. Dangerous." The two words slurred together, sounded like one long jumble. I fought against the stun, against her words. Against what she wanted from me.

"Right." With that, she fired one more stun blast and everything went black.

12

Ivy, Cerberus Territory, Canteen

"CANTEEN, MY ASS." The muttered thought slipped from my lips on a whisper that would not carry. I only had a few hours remaining of my bargain with Astra, and so I spent my time like every minute was made of gold. It took me eighty-three minutes from the moment I left Zenos behind to steal some explosives from Astra's storerooms and make my way back to the canteen I'd been to the night before. I had to hurry also because the stun on Zenos would only last so long. When he recovered, I had to be gone. Long gone.

A huge smile lit my face when I saw the specialty grenades. They were ReCon ordinance, designed to blow a compact hole through a wall. Just one wall, and just large enough to allow us to pass one fighter at a time. I had much experience with them. They were stolen, no doubt, from a Coalition ship so I felt no guilt whatsoever stealing them back. They were mine first, and I knew exactly how to use them.

I *did* want to take down Cerberus. I did *not* want to blow a hole in the airtight structures that protected the people living on this moon base above planet Hyperion. I'd learned much about the culture here, the people. They weren't wild like everyone thought. They were trying to live, to raise children, to be happy, just like everyone else in the universe. I would not mess with that.

I was only after one male now. One villain. One more bad guy. As I watched the canteen from the rooftop Zenos had pointed out last night, I realized something, or rather *remembered* something.

"Thought you had me fooled, didn't you, Cerberus?" Looking through the specially enhanced visor on my bounty hunting helmet, I watched with interest as the heated outlines of five workers moved about in an underground lab. The visor was one of my favorite toys. It made me feel like Superman, X-ray vision and all, even seeing below the ground.

"Thought I wouldn't notice?" I said to myself. "Too covered in the stench of Cerberus Legion blood?" Talking out loud to no one was the best indicator of my mental state, but I was beyond caring now. The night before, not one of the Cerberus Legion members that I'd taken down had smelled of alcohol nor behaved as if they were drunk, out to get lit and party hard. I'd been around enough dirty bars and backward canteens on the outskirts of Coalition-controlled space to know what the drink of choice smelled like on just about every planet. Here? Nothing.

But I *had* smelled something else.

Quell. Not on their breath, as I had with my unit, but on their clothing. In their hair.

Last night with Zenos, I'd been standing outside the bar —and then been inside. I wasn't so hyper-focused now and realized where I'd been—a huge Quell production laboratory—and had no idea.

I checked my uniform data. Midday. Several blocks away, the sounds of children playing and an active trading plaza drifted to me under the tall dome overhead. Over here at the canteen? It was like I was doing ReCon on a morgue. It was quiet, almost dead. The whole area was shut down.

Seemed even Cerberus didn't want to do what they did in front of their children.

Maybe a few of them were human, after all. Well, not human exactly, but perhaps not monsters either. I had to hope all of that meant that while Cerberus Legion was awful, their code extended to children. Left them out of it.

When Jillela walked out of the building, I allowed her to go. I *wanted* her to remain among the ranks. Clearly she had a line to Cerberus himself. I'd bested her in a fight, but I'd also taken down a hybrid Atlan in beast mode. She hadn't stood a chance against me. And that made her reasonable. Intelligent. Cerberus, the male who led the entire legion, he was an asshole, and he was going down. He'd known about Gerian Eozara, knew about the Quell production. Allowed it. Probably reaped the rewards himself. He was just as guilty as Gerian. Cerberus Legion was going to need Jillela's help to pick up the pieces and protect their innocents after I was finished today.

Cerberus, the leader, was going down. Cerberus, the legion, was going to change. I didn't know Jillela well, but I had to believe she was not as evil as her boss.

Before I settled on the rooftop, I'd gathered information from a male whose arm I'd twisted from his socket before I knocked him out. He'd shared that there truly was an underground lab as I'd thought and that Cerberus himself was there now.

I repacked my gear, careful of the explosives I carried, and made my way down and out of the building. Circling around a few blocks, I moved from shadow to shadow until I was at the rear of the building. There was no door, no windows, not on any of the levels. But I didn't need one. I was going to make my own.

Placing the first sticky grenade against the base of the wall, I set the timer for twenty seconds, ran and took cover.

Boom!

The sound ricocheted up and down the empty streets, and I knew I would have company soon. Lots of company.

"Bring it, assholes." Smiling from ear to ear when I saw the explosive had done its job, I stepped through the crumbling hole in the wall and ran for the next barrier. An elevator shaft. Sealed doors. Locked. The security was good, and I knew I wouldn't be able to crack the coding, even with my Hived-Up enhancements. Screw it. I had enough explosives to take down three buildings this size.

I set another charge, ran around the corner.

Boom!

I peeked around the edge of the wall. Yep. I'd made a nice big hole in the now non-functioning elevator doors. Perfect.

I pulled another explosive from my pack and tossed it down the elevator shaft.

When the explosion rumbled beneath my boots and a blast of flame and heat rushed past me, I tossed another one. The last probably took care of the elevator's ceiling and this one would fall inside the box and take care of the door.

One more blast and I knew it was time. It was like a video game. I had the weapons, I had the powers. It was time to seek out the enemy and finish them.

Pulling my blasters free from their holsters, I walked to the blown-to-bits elevator doors and looked down the smoke-filled elevator shaft. I had a moment to think that it was weird elevators were here on Rogue 5, just like on Earth. Similar primitive technology in so many ways. The only difference was the explosion part. I'd never had reason to blow up an elevator shaft on Earth. Here... I had plenty of reason.

It was time to finish this, once and for all.

Thanking God for the Hived-Up parts and pieces that made me more than human, I jumped down into the flames and faced the enemy.

———

Zenos, Astra Legion

"WHAT THE FUCK do you mean, Rhord is dead?" That wasn't possible. I'd just seen him a few hours ago. That, and he was a Forsian hybrid. Big. Tough. Hard to kill.

I was so angry at Ivy, using the stun setting to immobilize me. To get away. I'd only just recovered from it, my muscles and nerves reviving again from the powerful blocker. Before I could go after her, I'd heard of Rhord but had to learn the truth, so I'd come here.

Nev paced Astra's private quarters, his fangs fully extended in a killing rage. "Cerberus left his body at the tunnel entrance."

It was true.

Astra stood at the window of her tenth-story balcony. From here she could see all her territory and half of Cerberus Legion's streets as well. "You did say Cerberus wanted to rule all of Rogue 5."

I had. Fuck. "I didn't think he was stupid enough to challenge you, Astra."

She didn't turn from the window, her gaze pensive as the city's lights spread out like a sea of stars under the black dome that kept us safe. "Not only me. Styx and Kronos. They will not approve of this attack. Killing while a guest in another legion. This will destroy the balance of power on Rogue 5. It's bad for business."

Bad for business? It was worse than that. A blatant attack. He'd wanted Ivy, but this much? Enough to start a fucking war?

Nev growled, still moving as Barek approached our leader slowly, with more caution than I'd ever seen from him when standing close to her. "My lady—"

She stiffened but didn't look his way. "I told you not to call me that."

He stopped, bowed his head. "I'm sorry, Astra. Please, send us to avenge our fallen brother. Cerberus had no right."

She sighed and finally looked at him, her expression not unkind but filled with regret. "Agreed. He came into my territory wearing Cerberus colors. He was escorted under the guise of peace to a meeting, where he offered us a gift. This is unacceptable. Killing Rhord under these circumstances is an act of war."

My fists clenched at my sides as I agreed. With Ivy driving me mad with frustration, it would feel good to kill a few more Cerberus scum. "We will handle it for you, Astra. Send me, Barek and Nev. We'll gather a few Enforcers and hunt him down."

She didn't move, her gaze fixated once again on something in the distance. "Jillela will replace him. She is cunning but not cruel. Do not kill her. We need her alive."

"Agreed," Barek stated. He understood her strategy, her thinking about more than just Cerberus dead. That was why she was leader, considering the repercussions as part of the actual plan. Risk had to match the reward.

"Good. Let's fucking get out there and burn their house to the ground." Nev was the youngest of us, primed to fight, his instincts still difficult for him to control.

Astra tilted her head to the side as if puzzled, and an orange-hued light flashed over her skin.

"What was that?" Barek pulled the sheer fabric covering the window nearest him aside to look at the source of the unusual light.

Astra was smiling now. "It would appear that someone has beaten us to the task." She pointed out the window.

Dread dropped like a stone in my gut, cold and hard and immovable. No. Not Ivy. She'd stunned me to go after Cerberus. To finish her mission.

But even as I denied the thought, I knew I was wrong. I strode to the window. Ivy was out there. Alone. Not just out there, in *Cerberus* Legion.

"By the gods." Barek's reverent tone lured me to look at what I did not want to see.

Flames shot into the air on the roof of one of the buildings in Cerberus Legion. It was far in the distance, but that only meant it was more intense up close. Looking down over the city, I did some quick calculations and guessed that the building on fire had to be the canteen Ivy and I had visited yesterday.

"Why didn't you stop her?" Astra asked. "You should be with her."

I nodded, swallowed. "I should, but as you probably understand, a female has a strong mind and will let nothing get in her way."

"You mean no one."

I didn't reply because there was no argument. Ivy had fucking stunned me to get away.

A loud pounding sounded from Astra's door, the culprit shoving it open wide without waiting for a response from anyone within. "Astra, there has been a break-in."

"Where? What was taken?" She didn't turn away from the vision before her, apparently hypnotized by a piece of Cerberus's empire burning to the ground. I knew the biofilters would take care of the smoke under the dome, keep the rest of Rogue 5 from breathing too much of the toxic fumes, but I still didn't understand how Ivy could be responsible... even though my instincts screamed at me that it was so.

The messenger took a deep breath. "Weapons and explosives, Astra. Two ion blasters, top grade, the new ones. Ten ion grenades and a few other things."

Air trapped in my lungs, I stepped closer to the window, stared at the flames through the glass, knew they were reflected in my own eyes. A small army could use that much firepower. Or one Earth female with a death wish. "Ivy."

At last Astra turned to me, to Barek, to Nev, who had finally stopped pacing to join us at the window, forming a circle of giants around our leader.

Astra looked up at me. "What are you waiting for? Go get your mate, bring her back safe. I want her."

That made me pause. What was Astra saying? "We have not mated," I said, ensuring she did not misunderstand.

She shrugged. "She's yours."

I paused, considered. She'd been mine since I first saw her on Zenith. "You would offer her a place among the legion?"

Astra nodded. "I would. She's a beautiful, powerful weapon, Zenos. And she's a protector. While she's focused on revenge, she's gone off alone, ensuring no one from Astra is with her, to keep all of us safe. She has strength and power beyond anything we can imagine. We can't fight beside her because we're not skilled enough. No one is. If blood is going to flow, it will only be hers."

I didn't like what she was saying one fucking bit.

"She's also good with the children. Even Nero liked her. She's yours. She's *ours*, Zenos. We need her. I want her to stay."

"So do I," I admitted. I did. So fucking bad my insides felt like they were being ripped out as I watched a black plume of smoke grow in the distance.

I looked to Barek to gauge his reaction, but his gaze was carefully blank.

"Barek? Nev?"

Nev pumped his fist in the air. "Let's go."

———

Ivy, Cerberus Legion

THE ROOM FILLED WITH SMOKE, the air so thick with it that I had to rely on the uniform's helmet visor system to navigate around the basement. Of the few bodies I'd seen moving around down here, they all lay motionless now... all but one. Him. My enemy.

"Cerberus, where are you?" I shouted.

A melting piece of air duct fell from the ceiling with a large crash, crushing what looked like a steel workstation beneath its weight. It wasn't safe down here, but I didn't care. I was too close to avenging my true family to stop now.

"Cerberus? I know you're here. I followed you, you know. I've been watching you all day." It wasn't exactly true, but he didn't need to know that. Once I'd learned he'd entered this building, I'd watched his heat signature. I'd met him face-to-face, knew his size, his speed, the way he moved.

The others strewn about were dead already. But Cerberus? Somehow he'd survived the blasts and the smoke.

I intended to change that.

"So, Ivy, you've been watching me?" Cerberus stepped into view, barely. Smoke swirled between us, but I could see the outline of his form and I was sure he could see mine.

"Yes."

"I've been expecting you. Tell me, what did you think when I slit that pretty-boy Forsian hybrid's throat and left him for dead? You were particularly fond of him, I believe. Pity."

I staggered, the hit to my gut like a blowtorch, so much worse than anything I had been prepared for. More painful even than watching my foolish, pill-popping friends crash and die behind enemy lines. "What the hell are you talking about?"

His laughter was mocking. Cruel. "I'm everywhere, Earth human. You think you're the only one with extra abilities? I am Cerberus." He shouted the last, pounded his chest with his fist. "One down, three to go. Then Astra's territory is mine."

I'd underestimated him. Or I'd overestimated myself. I had the Hive tech. I was practically invincible, except for one way I'd never expected. There were no integrations to fortify your heart.

He'd killed Zenos? Slit his throat? Bile rose in my throat, and it felt as if one of those explosives had detonated in my chest. Blown up my heart.

"No."

He grinned. Jesus, he fucking grinned. "Yes, Ivy. Just like last time, you're too little, too late. You can't save him because all that's keeping his head attached to his body is his spine. No ReGen pod will save your hybrid. You didn't protect him. You can't protect any of them."

Something in me snapped as pain. Heartbreak. Loss. I'd felt all of that when my teammates had died, but this was different. Zenos was different. I'd wanted it all from him, even his bite. My heart longed for his bossy ways. The arguments. That was all gone now. I hadn't even had a chance to argue with him about the bite, to fight with him. To tell him to fucking get over it already. But no, I couldn't do that now.

I pulled both blasters and fired. Direct hits to his chest.

He laughed. He fucking laughed. The weapons had no effect. He had to have some kind of internal armor. Hive tech. Something I'd never seen before.

I was Hived-Up, but even I couldn't take direct fire at this close proximity. He was something more. And I didn't care.

Throwing my blasters to the side, I met his gaze. Held it. "I'm going to kill you with my bare hands."

He held up his, showing me he had no weapons. "I was hoping you'd say that."

My own words, thrown back in my face. I'd uttered those same words moments before I'd killed his people, members of his legion, people under his control and protection.

Cerberus launched himself at me, his body slamming mine with a staggering amount of weight. Too much, even for a male of his size. He knocked me back and I stumbled. I summoned every ounce of strength, calling on my Hived-Up enhancements to come to my aid. But it wouldn't. Not with a body blow like that. It was impossible to fight inertia, and I went down. I rolled, coming up to my knees, but he was right there.

His right arm swung wide, a boxer's haymaker punch, and I dodged it. The follow-up left hook hit me beneath the arm, cracking my ribs. I groaned, the air knocked from me.

I rolled, spun and lashed out, arcing a kick to his head. I heard the crack, felt it in my heel. It knocked him back, blood spurting from a wound at his temple.

He paused, blinked, and I took advantage, pulling out my knife, ready to slice his throat.

He growled, lunged, grabbed my wrist, knocked me back again. This time I fell to the floor, Cerberus pinning me. His grip was sure. Powerful and the knife clattered to the ground. He grabbed it, ready to slice out.

I pushed off, knocked him back so he was no longer upon me. We stared at each other, him with my knife. He was strong. Really strong. I was breathing hard, my ribs screaming. I'd fought dozens of males the night before without even blinking, but Cerberus? I now understood why he ruled the legion.

"You," I panted, eyeing him. "You didn't need to know who did my enhancements. You're already Hived-Up." The accusation burst from my lips as I realized I couldn't beat him. Not like this. He wasn't holding me down, but I might as well be pinned, at his mercy. He was going to kill me.

This wasn't an even fight. Cerberus had been humoring me all along, ever since he'd stood before me earlier in that meeting room. He didn't want me for his own—well, maybe he did if I'd have sworn allegiance—but instead wanted me dead.

"No, I don't need his help. But I do intend to kill him."

More blood on my hands. "Why?"

He laughed and the sound made my blood run cold. "There are already too many of us. And that idiot ruler of Prillon Prime is allowing the others on The Colony to return to their home planets. Stronger. Bigger. Faster. *Better.*"

He thought the fighters who'd been taken and tortured by the Hive were better? He was so evil.

"You don't want the competition," I said, trying to understand.

"I am a king, not a gladiator. I take what should be mine."

"You're insane." That was the truth, and I didn't care to hold my tongue. I was going to die down here in this fiery shithole anyway.

"Perhaps." He launched then, knocking me back once more. I groaned at the smack of my body against the hard ground, the weight and energy of Cerberus knocking the air from my lungs. Again. He held my hands pinned above my head, his body atop mine, holding me down on my back so I was helpless to do anything but stare up into his crazy eyes and hope for a miracle.

It had all come to this. Every waking moment—and my nightmares during sleep—were to avenge my teammates. Now I would be dead like them. Cerberus getting away with it all. They would have died for nothing. Their lives, for nothing. They mattered.

Me? I didn't matter. No one would remember me. Not on Earth. Not in the Coalition. Not on Rogue 5. One slice with the knife and it would be over.

"Go ahead and do it," I told him. "Kill me."

"My pleasure, Ivy." He pressed the business end of the knife to my throat.

I closed my eyes and squeezed the lids closed. Hard. Waited for the sharp point of the blade to slice and rend. To tear my flesh, my arteries and end me.

And then he was gone, ripped away from me as if a tornado had lifted him and tossed him across the room. An animal took his place, fangs extended, a roar like none I'd ever heard filling the space like the blast of a shotgun. He loomed, wild and untamed. Vicious.

"Zenos," I whispered. My heart soared. "You're alive."

The male I'd fallen in love with looked down at me, and I'd never been so happy, so insanely, out of my fucking mind happy to see anyone in my life. Yes, I loved him. God, did I. I'd thought my life was over, not because I hadn't been able to avenge my unit, but because I'd thought Zenos was dead. Why live when my heart was gone?

But he was here. Alive. And he'd just saved my life.

I sat up, watched as Zenos stalked to Cerberus. He plunged a fist into Cerberus's chest and I heard bones crack. Break. The leader fell to his knees. I saw Barek and Nev in the doorway. Watching. Waiting.

"You laid a hand on my female," Zenos said. He struck again. "Mine. I vowed to protect her." And again. "Don't fuck with what's mine."

And once more.

Cerberus was dead. Sprawled on the ground in a

basement with his chest caved in like a broken eggshell. No righteous ending.

It was over. My mission. My rage. My personal battle. It was all over.

When Zenos turned to me, helped me to my feet and looked me over for injuries, I realized I was staring at my life. My heart. It belonged to Zenos.

13

Ivy, Zenos's Personal Quarters, Astra Legion, Rogue 5

THE LIGHTS WERE SET to five percent, only a soft glow lit the bedroom, or sleeping room, as Zenos called it. Considering all we'd been through, the fact that I'd stunned him so he wouldn't come after me, we didn't say much after we returned from Cerberus Legion, or when we stripped our soiled body armor and showered, or when we slid beneath the cool sheets of his bed.

I'd thought he would yell at me, spank my ass as he'd often threatened to do. I deserved it, all of it. Perhaps I was emotionally vulnerable because I'd thought he was dead, that nothing really mattered except that he was breathing and whole.

Maybe he was quiet because he wanted to stun my ass for what I'd done.

Either way, we stayed quiet.

Cerberus was dead. He'd started a war, and we'd

finished it quickly. The Quell lab was destroyed, but so was the Cerberus Legion, from the top down. I couldn't believe the news that Rhord was dead, that Cerberus had killed him... out of retribution? Hatred? Just because he'd been an asshole without a little bit of integrity?

I felt all this, and I wasn't even a member of the Astra Legion. How dare he fuck with them? Sure, everyone from Rogue 5 had a bad reputation all over the galaxy, but others didn't understand. They didn't know them. Not really. I hadn't either until I arrived. Until I learned what they were really like. They might be rogue, but Astra Legion were good people. Like Robin Hoods of space where they might be outlaws, but they broke laws—or at least bent them—for good reason. They had an unspoken code of ethics that didn't get broken. Until Gerian Eozara. Until Cerberus went too far.

What he'd done would bring the legion closer together, not tear them apart as he'd wanted. They'd all be wary though. Jaded.

What Gerian Eozara did, how Cerberus had responded, showed why they had the code, why they stuck together, forged bonds that were as strong as those fighting the Hive.

It was good versus bad in the Wild Wild West of space.

I couldn't stop thinking about what had happened, that Gerian Eozara had been caught, that the Quell operation coming out of Cerberus was shut down. That Cerberus himself was dead. It was over. Justice hadn't been served—yet—because Gerian Eozara was still alive, but my job was done. He'd be tried for his crimes. Someone else would rule Cerberus Legion. Take on that name as their own. Hopefully make it become something honorable.

I wasn't stupid enough to think that Quell would never be distributed again. My team was still dead. They didn't care that he'd been captured or that Cerberus Legion was in turmoil. They didn't care about anything since they were fucking dead. I was still the only one who lived. I'd been so focused on getting retribution, getting revenge, that I'd lost track of what I really wanted. What I needed in life.

I wasn't a fighter any longer. Hell, I wasn't even fully human. My integrations made me so I couldn't go back to Earth, even if I wanted. I no longer had a mission, a job to do. I wasn't the same woman who'd volunteered. I wasn't the same woman who'd graduated from the Academy. I wasn't even the same woman who'd survived years of battle with the Hive. I was lost, it seemed, the only thing anchoring me was Zenos's arms about me.

The only place I found comfort, where I was accepted for exactly who I was, and what, was with Zenos. And I'd stun blasted his ass.

"I can practically hear you thinking," Zenos murmured, reaching across the bed and pulling me into him, my back to his front. One arm was slung over my waist, his palm resting on my belly, fingertips brushing the undersides of my breasts. He was warm, his muscles hard. Hard everywhere.

The prod of his cock at my back made my nipples pebble, my body warm.

God, I wanted him. Needed him. He was my own personal addiction. I craved how he made me feel. His touch was like a drug, the pleasure it gave me was insatiable.

I doubted I'd ever stop craving and knew I'd want only what he could give me.

It was simple, the need. My body knew exactly what it wanted: him. My heart wanted him, too. It was his. Solely, completely. I had no idea when I'd fallen in love with him. We argued enough for me to want to hit him with an ion cannon not set to stun, but somehow, between all the shouting and bickering, I'd given him my heart.

My mind though... was the only logical part of me. He might make me feel good, might have my love, but it wasn't enough. He'd made it clear that I wasn't enough for him.

Yeah, I was thinking too fucking hard.

"I'm sorry I stunned you."

He grunted at that, his hands gripping me tighter.

"When I saw him looming over you, knife to your throat... female, I aged ten years."

I didn't tell him I'd been about to die. That wouldn't have helped a thing.

"We agreed you wouldn't go off into danger alone."

"You said I couldn't go." I didn't want to argue. I was too raw. Too much had happened. I'd been too close to death, to understanding real loss. "It's over," I told him, staring at the plain wall. Talking about what had happened was so much easier than talking about my heart. "Gerian's in a cell, or whatever it's called on Rogue 5. He won't hurt anyone else ever again."

Zenos tensed behind me. "Yes. And Cerberus is dead. I am pleased to know it was by my hand."

I'd learned so much about the Astra Legion in the short time I'd been with them. The moon base was a strange place, their customs so different than Earth, than fighting in the Coalition.

I understood Zenos's frustration; I felt it, too. How the hell had I come to think of Astra Legion as a familiar place? As a home of sorts? I felt a kinship, a bond with everyone.

I understood it. I understood them.

For the first time in... forever, I'd felt like I belonged. Not just with Zenos but with Astra Legion. The camaraderie they shared was one I understood. They belonged to Zenos, and for some crazy reason that fact made them the family I'd never had. Never knew I was missing.

I rolled over to face Zenos, met his dark eyes, the gaze I'd thought I'd never see again. The hands I'd never feel on my body. His thumb stroked over my belly. We were so close our noses almost brushed. The hair on his chest tickled my already sensitive nipples. "Let's forget it all." Reaching down between us, I gripped his cock. "For tonight."

"Ivy," he groaned, his hips bucking into my tight stroke from root to tip. "I won't forget how you endangered yourself."

My eagerness wilted at his words. I could understand his anger, but why was he doing this now when I'd offered a truce? I was giving him a hand job!

"Are you trying to pick a fight?" I asked, letting go of him and pushing up to sitting. The sheet that had covered me fell to my waist. Zenos's gaze fell to my bare breasts. The air was cool, but my nipples hardened further by the look in his eyes, not the temperature.

"You risked your life," he countered. "I ordered you to stay back, but you wouldn't. You *stunned* me."

"I apologized. It will always be there between us, what happened."

"Ivy."

"Seriously, Zenos?" I stared down at him, wide-eyed. "I want to fuck, and you want to go all alpha? Now? Can't it wait for a little while?"

He turned onto his back, tucked his hands behind his head. "We will fuck. First, we talk."

I stared at him, thinking he was joking. When he did nothing but eye me back, I huffed. He wasn't joking.

"Fine," I snapped. "First, we talk." Then we get wild.

"Explain to me the integrations. Cerberus knew of them. Understood."

"He had them too."

Zenos's eyebrows shot up. That he had not known.

"That explains much about him. But you? Humans are weak and should not be able to fight as you did."

"I haven't been on Earth in several years and should be insulted by your statement for all mankind, but I'm not. We are weak and that's why I volunteered for the Coalition, to get the fuck off that planet."

"Very well, why are you not weak like your species? Because you sliced through three from Cerberus with one stroke. Took down dozens, leaped over a few and landed a great distance away. That is not normal human behavior or abilities. You had Hive integrations injected by a black market dealer," he stated.

"Yes."

He sat up so quickly he almost knocked me backward. "Why? Why would you choose to be contaminated?" His gaze was thunderous, his voice booming. Everyone in the Coalition had heard of the concept of having Hive nanobots and other technology surgically added to a body to enhance strength, speed, hearing and any number of other possibilities. It was forbidden, and all who voluntarily sought out such enhancements were considered vile. Traitorous.

I narrowed my gaze, poked him in the chest. "Contaminated?" I huffed. "Do not use that term. Do you know how insulting that is to all the fighters out there captured, tortured and integrated? It makes it sound like what they suffered is something pleasant, something they wanted, like going to the mall to get your ears pierced."

He took a deep breath, let it out. "I do not understand

what you mean by going to a mall, but for the rest I apologize. You are correct. While we from Rogue 5 do not serve in the Coalition, I would never disrespect anyone their service or sacrifice, especially those who survived the Hive."

I nodded at his very sincere response.

"But why the fuck would you want Hive integrations?"

"I fought the Hive for four years. I told you about the battle that killed my unit." He nodded, so I continued. "You saw the scars. I was trapped on that planet for weeks. Alone. No medical help. After they found me, a ReGen pod only fixed small things. A broken finger, burns. But it couldn't fix everything. I was medically discharged from the Coalition. They did everything they could, but I couldn't make myself whole. I wasn't strong enough to fight or join a new ReCon unit. Every step I took was a battle and I knew I couldn't go after Gerian like that. My body was weak and I was in constant pain. The only difference between me and my unit was that I was alive. And they weren't in pain."

He set a hand on my knee.

"I was angry, had survivor's guilt. I hurt. I did what I had to do to be strong again. To fight. To track down whoever was responsible for selling my unit that damn drug."

"The implants made you stronger. Faster." The hand on my knee moved, petting me like I was a kitten. So gentle. I wanted to curl up in his lap and purr. "Are you still in pain?"

I shrugged. "Sometimes. But I can live with that. The integrations made me whole. They called me a rogue. Hived-up scum. But I didn't care what they called me back in the Fleet. If the Coalition's technology couldn't fix me, I was going to use other technology to do so. It was for the Coalition, and for my unit that I did it."

He shook his head. "You're not rogue, you're a rebel."

I shrugged again. "The end result is that I'm everything I wasn't before."

He took my wrist and tugged me down on top of him so we were chest to chest. "Don't you see? You are one of the strongest people I know. And the implants have nothing to do with that. It's your heart. You've always been Ivy Birkeland from Earth. Your sense of honor, of loyalty has always been there. You're you."

His hand stroked up and down my back, and I knew he could feel the line of my scar.

I frowned, set a fist on his chest and rested my chin on it so I could look at him. "You sound like the Wizard of Oz telling Dorothy she'd had the way to get back to Kansas inside her the whole time."

His dark gaze roved over my face. "You have this fascination with this place called Kansas. I should like to see it one day."

I smiled, realizing I liked referencing that old movie.

"I am sorry the same technology was inside Cerberus, but you ended him. He can't use it any longer for bad shit." I paused, took a breath, sneaked a glance at him through my lashes. "Have we talked enough?" I asked. "I want you and I want you now."

In one swift move he had us flipped so I was on my back, and he loomed over, his body pressing me into the soft mattress.

14

enos

I KISSED HER, craving her taste, the feel of my lips claiming her mouth, a promise of what my cock would soon do with the plunge of my tongue.

Fuck, I wanted to rage at her, yell at her. Tie her to my bed so she'd never put herself in danger again. Spank her. Fuck her. Kiss her. *Love her.*

Feelings pumped through me at what had happened. At what had *almost* happened. But I couldn't think of it, wouldn't or I'd go insane. Ivy was here, with me, beneath me. Gerian Eozara would be sent to a Coalition court. Cerberus was dead. Thank fuck.

And Ivy was mine. I had the rest of my life to shout and argue with her.

My forearms held me aloft, keeping the bulk of my weight from crushing her, yet I felt all her soft curves. One knee bent and she slid her leg along my thigh and hip. The action had me settling at her core, my cock pressed into her wet heat.

Fuck, she felt good. She smelled good. She tasted good. I loved everything about her. Except for her wild streak where she acted rashly and impulsively. I hadn't been joking when I'd seen her beneath Cerberus, ready to have her throat slit. Her Hive tech hadn't saved her then, but when she'd said he'd had it too, fuck.

No, don't think. Revel in Ivy.

She was where she belonged, here on Rogue 5 with me. In my arms. Beneath me. It was the only place I knew where she was safe. Whole. I never wanted to let her up, to let her go.

I never expected to find a perfect match. I hadn't been tested, but if I'd participated in the Interstellar Brides Program, there was no doubt the computer would have put us together.

She'd been made for me. Every sassy, wild, rebellious inch of her.

I kissed along her jaw, sucked at the lobe of her ear, nuzzled her neck. I worked my way down her body until I got to her breasts. Fuck, they were full, soft, and the tips were so responsive. Sensitive. I played there until she writhed beneath me, her skin damp with sweat, her cries cutting through the silence of my sleeping room.

I couldn't get enough. My cock seeped pre-cum like a waterspout, my balls ached to be emptied. And my fangs.

Fuck, my fangs dropped and wanted to nip at the turgid tip, to have her fingers tangle in my hair, her back arch.

My fangs wanted to taste her sweet skin, then pierce it. Mark her permanently as mine.

No. NO! I couldn't. I wouldn't do that to her. I loved her too much.

I paused, my mouth hovering over her navel.

I loved her. That was why I was so fierce with her. So angry and frustrated with her wild spirit, all the while secretly thrilling in it.

I wanted Ivy Birkeland from Earth as my own. Forever. Always.

Completely.

"Zenos," she whispered, her hands on my head, reminding me of where I was and where I was going.

She could be mine, all except for the bite. I couldn't do it to her. We had the antidote with the scientists. She'd taken it. Even so, I couldn't do it. I couldn't risk it, us. Her.

I could survive without the connection biting her would bring. I'd lived this long without it, I could keep going. I would survive without claiming her. But I couldn't— wouldn't—live without her.

She would die. Die! I'd almost lost her earlier, and I wouldn't risk it again, not by my own hand. Or fangs. I was fierce about her safety, especially now that I'd witnessed her fighting so valiantly against Cerberus. She was stronger than I ever imagined, yet that battle had proven her nearly invulnerable. It seemed the only danger left to her was... me.

"Zenos," she said again, breaking me from my thoughts.

I looked up her bare body, grinned into her blue eyes.

"You want my mouth on your pussy?" I asked, licking at the skin over her hip bone. "You want to come just as you did that first time on Zenith?"

She nodded, pushed my head down toward her core. "Please."

"Ah, you beg so beautifully. The difference between then

and now is that we have all the time in the world. I shall make you come. Make you scream my name. Only then will you get my cock. That shall be your punishment for stunning me. The sweetest torture."

"Shut up and do it already," she snapped.

Ah, my wild one. Fiery, fierce and greedy.

I did as she wanted and flattened my tongue, licked a path up her slit, then used my thumbs to part her, to open her up. She whimpered. I went to work, licking and flicking her clit, slipping a finger into her pussy to find the little ridge of flesh that made her gasp and jerk, pressing my thumb to the tight ring of her ass.

I knew when she was close to coming, for her pussy gushed, her thighs clenched and her fingers tightened in my hair. Several times I pulled away, kissed her inner thigh, grazed the tender skin with my fangs. Then returned to push her to the brink again.

She was lost. Wild. Completely abandoned to the pleasure I wrung from her body. The desperation. The need.

I was powerful in this moment, my face covered in her essence, the taste of her on my tongue, the greedy grip of her inner muscles working my fingers. Teasing me with what it would be to feel her body surround my cock. Like a hot, wet fist.

"Zenos!" she cried in frustration. Her foot, which had been on the bed, her legs parted wide around my shoulders, lifted and whacked me in the back of the head. "Stop being an asshole and make me come. Otherwise I can do it myself."

I grazed my teeth over her swollen, sensitive clit.

"Zenos!" she growled in response to my silent warning.

I flicked her clit, curled my fingers that were in her pussy and breached her back entrance with a wet finger all at the same time. That was all it took for her to come, that triple gesture. I'd held off until now, until she was beyond reason. Why? Because I could. Because I wanted her to know what it was like to be at someone else's mercy. To suffer. Because I knew in that instant she was mine completely. Under my control. My spell.

And yet the sounds of her orgasm, the feel of her body as it succumbed, the taste of her... everything, made me weak. Vulnerable. Because this was everything and it could be taken away. I was powerful, yet completely powerless to Ivy Birkeland of Earth. I would do anything and everything I could to make her happy. Whole. Mine.

Except bite her.

Her body wilted into the bed, her breathing ragged. I smiled, content to see her so blissful. I'd done this to her. My cock throbbed, patient for this long but unable to hold off a moment longer from sinking into her.

I crawled up her body, nudged her thighs wide with my knee, found her entrance with the broad crown of my cock and slid home.

Yes, home. In her, with her was where I belonged. Where she was, I was. Where she began, I ended. Buried deep, we were one.

My fangs ached to sink into her as well. My mating fist wanted to swell, to lock us together. The basest biological instincts in my DNA called to me in this moment to mate with her. I wanted to. Fuck, I wanted it more than anything in the world. No, not anything. There was only one thing I wanted more.

Ivy.

I began to move, to fuck, to give her my cock and my body. To take from her as she took from me.

I wasn't going to last, she felt too good. After the battle

with Cerberus, I needed this connection, needed to know she was whole and healthy, safe and protected.

I saw the throbbing pulse at her neck, my mouth watered for more of her taste.

I craved the desire to sink into her soft flesh with more than just my cock.

"Zenos," she murmured. A hand hooked behind my neck, and I met her gaze. My hips continued to thrust, to push us higher and higher, closer and closer to the joint pleasure we would find. "Bite me."

Her words were like an ice bath, numbing my desire. I couldn't. I shook my head, continued to fuck her but without the mindless abandon.

"Bite me," she repeated, her words harsher, more insistent.

I dropped my forehead to the pillow beside her, breathed in her scent. "No."

She stilled. "What?"

"I'll give you everything else. Someone's blood on my hands. My protection. My cock. I'll give you my seed. I'll give you more pleasure than you can imagine, but I won't give you my fangs."

Her hands went to my chest, and she pushed me up. I planted my palms on either side of her head, stilled my hips, but remained deep inside her.

"What is it?" I asked.

"You won't claim me?" Her voice was small, so unlike her.

I was inside her, and yet I felt her withdrawal, felt her emotionally pull away from me.

"No. I can't."

She pushed even harder, and I sat back on my heels. My

hands cupped the back of her thighs, held myself in her. If she slid up the bed, I would come out of her pussy.

"You mean you won't."

"Same thing," I replied.

Turning to her side, she moved so I did slip from her. She climbed from the bed. She had red marks on her pale skin where I'd kissed and licked, sucked and grabbed. Her arousal coated her inner thighs. Her nipples were hard points. Her cheeks were flushed, her damp hair a wild tangle.

"It's completely different." She paced the room, looking down at the ground. All at once she turned and left the room.

I followed her to the bathing room. She'd been searching for her clothes. They were in a pile on the floor.

"What are you doing?" I asked. I was still aroused, my cock hard and dark with my blood. Engorged. Glistening with her pussy juices. Pre-cum oozed from the slit.

"I'm getting dressed. What does it look like I'm doing?" she snapped.

"Why?"

"I don't know how many times I have to say the same thing. I won't die from your bite."

I shook my head. "I won't risk it." I ran my hand through my hair.

"There is no risk." She looked to me, her eyes bleak. "You don't trust me."

"I don't trust *me*," I countered, setting my hand on my bare chest. "I won't risk it. I almost lost you once today. I won't risk it again."

She tugged her shirt over her head, stalked out and straight for the exit. The door slid silently open, and she stepped out. Turning on her bare heel—she hadn't put on her underwear, only her shirt and pants—she stood before me, her face emotionless. Flat.

"You already did."

With those three words, she slapped her hand on the exterior wall and the door closed between us.

15

"I'M SENDING this comm to notify you that Gerian Eovara, of Cerberus Legion, Rogue 5, has been captured. He was running a Quell production lab. Sending vids now." I looked to the comm tech and nodded. He did some fiddling with the controls in front of him, sending the recordings Barek and Nev had taken in the destroyed lab. I'd learned early on that the Coalition wanted proof to claim any bounty, and I would not let something like lack of proof or evidence of capture make this one null and void.

This bounty, the destruction of the lab and Cerberus's death closed the case on my unit. It brought finality to the Coalition, which they liked. With proof. They would contact my teammates' next of kin and let them know justice had been served. Perhaps it would bring them closure to what happened to their loved one, or at least allow them to grieve knowing the perpetrator was no longer free to harm others.

As for me, I felt no closure as I'd expected. I'd been driven these long months for it, so the pain at the loss of my friends would go away. The pain and suffering I'd survived had been for something. That my remaining alive had been for something.

Lately I'd thought I'd survived because I was meant to be with Zenos, to live on Rogue 5 and be a part of Astra Legion. To belong. With one word from my lover, that had been shot to hell.

No.

Zenos wouldn't bite me. Wouldn't claim me as his. He didn't believe the tests that had been conducted that proved the serum would work. He didn't trust me with the truth. Didn't love me enough to believe in me, to believe in us. I couldn't remain here. I felt like an Earth mistress, a woman a guy would fuck but not commit to. I'd never wanted commitment before, but I'd never met Zenos before. Never realized what he meant to me until I thought him dead.

I'd never been in love. I hadn't known what I was missing. And now I did, because it was so close, so attainable, especially the night before. Zenos had been deep inside me, his head right beside my neck. He only had to turn, sink his fangs deep into my shoulder. Somehow a mating fist would have swelled and locked us together, the combination of fangs and fucking would have been a claiming. A hybrid Forsian marriage of sorts.

So close, but never further away from a true bond.

Fuck that. Fuck the Coalition. Fuck everything. I was a rebel. Wild. Free. A fucking bounty hunter. I'd been alone all my life. I could remain alone. It would hurt, but it was better than being unloved.

That was why I'd walked out. I couldn't have slept in his bed, in his arms, knowing it was less than everything. I'd found someone in the hallway and asked him to find me empty quarters for the night. He'd been courteous—I was somewhat infamous within the legion—and took care of me. I'd climbed into the cold bed, cried. Sleep wouldn't come, but surety of what I had to do next had.

If Zenos didn't want me, then I wasn't staying. I'd take care of the bounty and be gone.

Astra came through the door into the comm room. Behind her was Gerian Eozara, primitive chains restraining his wrists and ankles. Behind him were Barek and Nev, ion pistols raised and ready to use. The prisoner was remarkably sedate, and I had to wonder if they'd stunned him into compliance.

I tilted my head toward the comm screen. "This is Elite Hunter Sabir with the I.C. He's the contact for external projects."

Astra's pale brow went up. "He handles the off-the-record investigations."

"Exactly."

The guy on the comms was Everian. He was serious, his gaze intense. Not like Zenos when he looked at me with unflinching arousal, but with a seriousness indicative of an I.C. operative.

"This is Astra of Astra Legion."

She nodded at the screen, then stepped to the side.

"And that is Gerian Eozara. You received the vids?" I asked.

His gaze dropped, and I knew he was reviewing what had been sent through. "Yes. Excellent work. The Coalition is pleased to hear about the capture and the termination of that channel of Quell production."

"The lab is destroyed. Not only do you have a prisoner,

but the leader of the Cerberus Legion is also dead," I told him.

"I see. Well done, Lieutenant."

So official. So formal. So without feeling. He didn't know my team, didn't know their names, their lives, anything. He didn't know how I'd been left for dead. How I'd been discharged from service. Well, he knew about that but didn't care, and still called me by my rank. There were hundreds, thousands... fuck, tens of thousands of fighters out there. Too many to care about. Or he was just too jaded.

"I shall send the transport coordinates, and the prisoner can be immediately sent."

Something distracted the Everian, and he spoke to someone off-screen. He moved to his right, and someone joined him.

"I am Dr. Helion, commander of the I.C., Lieutenant Birkeland. I commend you for your actions in bringing Gerian Eovara to justice and the toppling of the Cerberus Legion." He wore a dark green uniform, indicating he was in the medical field. I wondered how the Prillon was the head of the I.C. but in the health services. Actually I didn't give a shit.

"I'm not a lieutenant any longer," I countered.

"I have reviewed the vids of the destroyed lab, and I have to say, Lieutenant, that your performance was exemplary." He cocked his head to the side. "Yet you're human. Like my other favorite operative. She is small, like you. From Earth."

"I have no doubt you have all the information you need about me on your screen."

If he knew my rank, he knew my connection to the killed unit, to the crash, to my discharge. To the fact that I was from Earth. Everything. Just not how a human could pretty much lift the weight and heft of a refrigerator without breaking a sweat—or her back—and take out a dozen wild hybrid Hyperions with ease.

"The bounty is yours, Lieutenant. Well-earned."

He was fucking baiting me with my rank. I hated it, but I refused to fall for his continued ploy. He was an asshole, plain and simple. I didn't need to do more than look at him to know he was calculating. The I.C. had put a bounty out, which meant they were willing to go beyond the bounds of Coalition rules to track down Gerian. Helion played outside the rules to get desired results and used those results to his advantage. Like right now, with me.

"I would like to offer you something besides the bounty."

And here it was. "What a surprise." I crossed my arms over my chest, remained patiently silent.

He ignored my remark. "Your record with the Coalition was exemplary until the crash. Your discharge was honorable. It is evident you have more than recovered from your wounds. I am willing to offer you a new commission, Lieutenant. I need good people like you. I need you back in the Coalition."

"Working for the I.C.?" I clarified.

"Correct."

"And what would I be doing exactly?"

"You will go where I need you. You will have the latest technology, shuttles, support, everything you could possibly need at your disposal."

"You want a bounty hunter?" I asked.

"That would be a waste of your skills. I need someone who can operate behind enemy lines. Someone even the Hive will fear."

I thought of how I'd fought against Cerberus. Wild, pretty much unhinged. I'd used my newfound integrations to my advantage, killed the legion members without mercy. Without thought. I had almost died at his hand.

Yeah, I was a fucking mess. But I was also free.

"You want an assassin, then. One you control."

"If you want to call it that."

"I'm to return to the Coalition and do your bidding? Be your puppet? No, thanks."

"No?" Helion asked. From the tenseness of his jaw I could tell he wasn't used to being told no.

"No," I repeated. "Not interested."

"You're going to remain a bounty hunter, roaming the universe and taking on contracts that may or may not support you when I can offer you so much more?"

"That's right."

"You are skilled. Experienced. You should be where you could be of most use. You should help us win this war. Protect the Coalition. Protect Earth. Protect your people."

I turned and looked to Astra.

"I am."

Her eyes flared, and she nodded.

She understood what I hadn't said aloud, that I wanted to be a part of Astra Legion.

"Lieutenant," Helion said, the one word laced with a tone used for kindergarten teachers who were disappointed in five-year-olds.

"I'm not interested, Helion. I'm saying it in English, but I'm sure your NPU will allow you to comprehend in any language. I'm not interested in working for the I.C., and I'm not interested in the bounty on Gerian. You can keep your money."

His eyebrow went up in a small show of surprise. "You don't want your bounty?"

I sighed. "You run the entire I.C.?" I questioned. "Really? I wanted justice for my crew. I got it. I won't put a price on their lives. The bounty does. If you want to give it to someone, split it among my team's families. They deserve it."

I looked to Astra. "I brought in Gerian. Shut down the lab. Finished Cerberus. I did what I set out to do. The help from you and your legion was instrumental. For that, I thank you. For that, the prisoner is yours."

Helion understood what I was saying. "Lieutenant!" he snapped.

I didn't turn back to face him but said, "Watch as justice is served, Helion."

Astra pulled a blade from some hidden place in her boot and swung. With one swift and efficient slice, Gerian Eozara was cut open. Blood sprayed across the comm room's walls as the male dropped to the floor, dead before he hit the hard surface. Barek and Nev didn't even flinch, just watched as the blood spread.

Only then did I look back to the comm screen. "Got that, Helion? You will serve as witness. Rogue 5 justice has been served to Gerian Eovara. To my unit. Give the money to their families. It's over."

I could tell he was pissed. Beyond furious. "Work for me."

God, it was as if blood lust aroused him. That made him want me even more for his team. My ruthlessness in allowing Astra to finish Gerian Eozara only made me more of a commodity. It showed I was as heartless as he.

No, that wasn't the case at all. I'd given my heart to Zenos, but he'd refused it. I was numb to love. Perhaps that was the same thing to Helion. But I wouldn't go and do someone's bidding just because my heart got sliced from my chest with the same ruthless precision as Astra's blade through Gerian Eozara.

I'd offered myself completely to Zenos. I would give myself to no one else.

"As they say on Earth, bite me."

I reached out and slapped the comm tech's controls, ending the call.

Astra was smiling as she cleaned her knife.

"That can be arranged, you know," she said. "Because of you and your antidote."

With her free hand she hooked her fingers in the collar of her shirt, pulled it to the side. There, at the juncture of her neck and shoulder, were two angry red dots. I immediately recognized them as bite marks. I looked from her to Barek, who had a ridiculously smug expression on his face.

There was a dead hybrid Hyperion whose blood was spreading across the floor at our feet, and yet Astra and Barek looked as pleased as could be.

"You... the two of you, I mean, you're claimed?" I asked Astra.

She had to be at least fifteen years older than me, her time for finding true love should have happened a long time ago. And yet it hadn't happened until now. Until the antidote.

Barek stepped over the body and put his arm around Astra.

"Yes," Astra said. I'd never seen her look so... happy. "I've wanted him for so long, but without the antidote it was impossible."

"Until now," Barek added, smiling. He was actually... beaming.

I was happy for them, so happy.

"Zenos can claim you now."

I shook my head, the smile slipping from my face. "No. He doesn't love me. He won't claim me."

"What?" Astra asked, confused. "Why isn't he here with you?"

Had she just realized he was missing?

"Because he isn't *with* me. I don't belong to him. I never will."

Her eyes widened. "He won't bite you."

I shook my head. "No. He doesn't trust me."

Her lips thinned. She glanced up at Barek, then back at me. "You're leaving."

"Yes. With your permission I will transport to Zenith. I love it here. I love Astra Legion, how you made me belong. How I feel like one of you. But I won't stay and be less than everything to Zenos."

"I understand," Astra said. "Go with my permission. With the thanks of everyone in the legion. You may not remain on Rogue 5, but you are one of us." She set her hand over her heart. "In here."

Fuck, she might as well have stabbed me with her blade, it hurt that much.

I blinked, nodded, then left, headed for the transport room.

And the rest of my life.

enos

"Fᴜᴄᴋ," I whispered, my throat dry as the desert planet of Trion. I felt like shit. My head pounded, my mouth tasted as if I'd licked the backside of a sweaty Hyperion. I didn't usually drink to excess, but last night had called for it. Ivy had walked out on me. Not just walked out, she'd pushed me off her and left mid-fuck. Mid-fuck!

I was so blinded by my need to come that I'd watched her dress and then leave. My cock had been hard, throbbing, my balls aching with the obsessive need to fill her.

But she was gone. Her pussy was not where I'd spurted my cum. No, it had been into my hand as I'd stood there and stared at the door. I'd only tugged a few times, and I'd cupped the crown and had the hot fluid fill my palm. The release had been incredible, but it had been lacking. The hot, tight feel of Ivy's pussy, the way her inner walls milked me.

Only when I'd taken the edge off had I been able to think clearly. Ivy had been pissed at me. When wasn't she mad at me about something? We fought more than we fucked. It was our way. I hadn't gone after her because I had no intention of repeating the same old argument.

I wasn't biting her.

I loved her too much to risk her life. I was willing to sacrifice the need to claim her fully so I could see her smile. To hear her screams of pleasure. Fuck, even to bicker with her.

She was an obsession. Ever since I'd first laid eyes on her across the bar at the Transport Station Zenith, I craved her. She was my drug.

But I couldn't give her what she wanted. No, biting her would never happen.

I'd gone to the S-Gen machine and ordered up the strongest alcohol possible and drank it until I must have passed out. I woke on my bed, still naked, my hand gripping the base of my throbbing cock, my fangs descended. Even in my sleep I wanted Ivy. My body couldn't go hours without fucking her.

I climbed from bed and used the shower tube—emptying my balls again—and ran a fucking ReGen wand over my head to ease the throbbing. It surprised me Ivy had yet to return, to come in and tell me off with that sharp tongue of hers or push me onto the bed and use me for her needs.

Her mission was complete. She'd found Gerian Eozara, the secret lab, even, fuck, Cerberus, avenged the death of her fellow fighters. It would take a while to get over the hatred toward Cerberus, but I had his death to remember, to know justice was served for what happened to Rhord, to all of us. And Gerian would be dead as well, the Coalition executing those who harmed their own. We all had Ivy to thank for rooting him out. For ending it all.

She'd not only worked her way into my heart, but she'd worked her way into the legion itself. She was like us. Gods, she belonged here, not only with me but with all of Astra Legion. She might not be born on Rogue 5, but she was one of us.

And she was mine. She would come to understand how it would be. She would stop questioning, stop pushing for more than I could give. It seemed she didn't understand how much I loved her, no matter how many times we fucked, how often I showed her with my body. And that was the problem that I would fix now.

I would tell her how I felt. Show her again. And again. Until she believed me.

I dressed, left my quarters in search of Ivy.

I followed the scents of food and the sounds of voices to the dining hall. When I entered, there were about twenty or so eating their morning meal. I scanned the space. No Ivy. I did see Astra, who was smiling.

Smiling. What. The. Fuck?

I stalked over to her, dropped into an empty chair.

"What's the matter?" I asked. I rarely saw our leader's mouth turned up in amusement, let alone a full-on grin.

"What do you mean?" she asked. She glanced to Barek, who sat beside her as usual. What wasn't usual was the way he was looking at her. I was used to him watching her closely, fiercely. Now his gaze held the same possessiveness as always, but a... tenderness.

I scratched my head, wondering if I still had alcohol in my blood.

"You're smiling," I told her, then pointed at Barek. "What the fuck's got into you?"

He tipped his head back and laughed. My mouth fell open.

"Nothing's gotten into me, but I got into her." He looked to Astra and stroked her hair.

I couldn't believe it, but Astra actually blushed, her cheeks turning a bright shade of pink.

I glanced around the room at the others, no one paying us any attention, as if the moon base hadn't shifted off its axis.

I leaned forward, rubbed my temples. "Will you please fucking tell me what's going on? Why you're so damned happy all of a sudden? It can't be because Gerian Eozara is in the brig. Is there an update about Cerberus?"

"Gerian is dead," Astra said plainly. "Jillela will take over Cerberus. I'm sure of it. And I'm happy because of this."

She yanked the collar of her shirt to the side, and I saw the marks.

Barek's mark.

I stared. Then stared more at the red flesh.

He'd been in love with her for years. Decades. He'd never once touched her. As far as I knew, they'd never spoken of how they felt. How their love was unrequited.

Until now.

Until the antidote.

"It works." The words fell from my lips as I thought them.

"It works," Astra repeated.

"It sure as fuck does. Astra might be leader of the legion, but she's mine. Marked and claimed."

"Holy fuck," I whispered, then stood. My chair slid across the floor. My hands went to my hips. "You're telling me the antidote works? That we have it, the serum that will save us?"

Barek nodded but didn't look away from Astra.

I felt relief, happiness, so many things all at once. I dropped back into the chair, my legs giving out. We'd found it. We could mate. Have children. Keep our loved ones alive.

I popped back up again as if I were some child's toy bouncing up and down. "Ivy," I said, looking around again. "Where's Ivy?"

"Gone." Astra said the one word with such finality my head whipped around to look down at her.

"What do you mean, gone?"

Barek slowly stood, faced me. "Don't speak to my mate in such a tone," he growled.

Yeah, the antidote worked.

"I want to claim Ivy. Fuck, it works."

"You're too late," Barek said.

"What the fuck are you talking about?"

"She told you all along, since we were on Zenith even, that she'd taken the antidote and you could bite her. She told you to do it. You refused."

"Of course I refused. I didn't want her to die."

"She wouldn't have died," Barek countered.

"How would you know?"

Barek tipped his chin down. He was calm as fuck, and I was coming out of my skin.

"Because Astra is alive. She took the serum and I bit her and she didn't die."

"Obviously," I snapped, waving at a very serene Astra. Gods, a few orgasms and our leader went all soft.

"I trusted the tests that were done. I trusted Ivy that the antidote worked."

"You were willing to risk Astra's life?" I asked, stunned.

"I was willing to risk my life for Barek," Astra said. "For love. To finally belong to him."

"You could have died!" I shouted. Heads swiveled in our direction, the room went quiet.

Astra slowly stood. Barek moved to her side as if they were magnets and nothing could keep them apart.

"We have the antidote, Zenos. What we've wanted all along. You were too afraid to use it, to believe in it."

"I love her too much," I admitted. "I won't have her dead!"

"Then you won't have her at all," Astra added. "She's transported off Rogue 5. You refused to bite her, even with the antidote. You didn't trust her."

"Of course I trust her! I love her!"

I was repeating myself, I knew it. But I was irrational. Angry. She was gone?

Astra took a step toward me. "We've wanted the antidote all our lives. Generations before us would have killed for it. Now we have it. It's ours, Zenos. And yet you're still afraid to live, to claim the one you love. You must trust in Ivy. If you don't, your love means nothing."

I looked at the sickeningly in love duo before me.

They'd waited decades to mate. As soon as the antidote was available, they'd taken it. Not blindly, for it had been tested, but with faith nonetheless. They'd been willing to risk it all. For love.

But I hadn't. And now Ivy was gone. I'd given her everything she wanted except one thing.

Me. Completely. Blind faith. Blind trust.

"Fuck this shit," I muttered, spinning on my heel and storming off.

I'd had Ivy from the moment I first laid eyes on her. She'd been safe to claim with my fangs and cock. Willing.

Perfect. And I'd blown it. At first she hadn't wanted the bite, not wanting to be mated, but that had changed. She'd asked, begged even, for me to do it. She'd wanted to be my mate and I'd refused.

No longer. I stormed into the transport room, scared the hell out of the tech.

"Where did Ivy Birkeland of Earth go?"

His wide eyes indicated he was surprised and a touch afraid of me. "Transport Station Zenith."

"Send me there. Now."

I took the steps to the raised platform two at a time, determined to claim my female. Fangs and all.

———

IVY

Finding a bounty wasn't anything like going to the 7-11 and looking at the job board by the bathrooms. There was no tear-off phone number to call. I'd have to reach out to Elite Hunter Sabir again, and I had a pretty good feeling I'd burned that bridge. I had no doubt that when I ended that comm call, he'd gotten his ass chewed out by Helion. I'd brought in Gerian Eozara, just as the bounty had said. It had also stated dead or alive, so letting Astra finish the asshole didn't break the terms. I'd even had Sabir and Helion witness it. There was no question their own eyeballs were enough evidence.

That didn't mean they'd want to work with me again. I'd gone rogue. And that was a fucking hoot.

I tugged the blanket over my body, stuffed it under my arms, stared at the ceiling of the small quarters I'd been given on Zenith. I had nowhere to go, not until I had something to do.

Earth was out. No fucking way.

I could crawl on hands and knees to Helion and grovel —a lot—and he'd probably give me a job. He'd get what he wanted, a superpower Earth female. But I'd rather stay in this backwater transport station slinging drinks than beg him for a job.

Yeah, I'd totally gone rogue. I huffed and flopped onto my side.

I thought of Astra Legion, of my never-knew-existed-until-now home. It was home, definitely. The people there, I understood, and it seemed they understood me. They didn't care if I was a little wild, totally impulsive, loudmouthed, intense, bossy and even completely uncontrollable.

I was just like them.

I was wanted.

By every single member of Astra but one.

Zenos.

I rolled to my other side, kicked the blankets off in annoyance.

No, he wanted me. His cock didn't lie. But he didn't want me enough.

I put my fingers to my neck where it was unmarked. Unscarred. I hadn't wanted the scar that ran the length of my spine, but I did want one at my neck. One I would be proud to show off, because it meant I was loved. I belonged to him. With him.

Someone pounded on the door, and I sat up, pushed my hair back from my face.

"Go away!" I shouted, then flopped back in bed.

The pounding started up again.

"Go. The. Fuck. Away!" I yelled at the ceiling.

An ion blast and the opening of the door had me popping up and onto my knees.

"What the—"

Zenos came in, ion pistol raised. He stopped just inside the room, legs spread wide, gaze squarely on me.

He was the hottest thing I'd ever seen. But that meant nothing.

"What the fuck are you doing here?" I snapped.

He reached his arm out, slapped the wall, and the door closed behind him, not silently since his ion shot must have done something to the inner mechanism.

"I'm here for you. I'm thinking I should stun you to keep you from running off. Sound familiar?"

I arched a brow. "Oh really?"

He said nothing.

"You here for another quick fuck?"

He stepped to the edge of the bed. "Yes."

I sat back on my heels, deflated. "Not happening. Not offering."

I was in my shirt and panties, I'd ditched my pants and boots on the floor.

"You've offered what I want since the first time I saw you."

"It's off the table. My pussy's not available."

He opened his mouth, and I cut him off with a raised hand.

"Neither is my ass or mouth, so don't even think it."

He reached out, grabbed my upper arm and pulled me back up onto my knees. With his free hand, he tucked my long hair back over my shoulder, slid a finger down the length of my neck.

"While appealing, that's not what I had in mind."

I swallowed, took in his gorgeous face. His dark eyes

were on my pulse point. His jaw was clenched. His grip, while sure, was gentle.

"What... what did you have in mind?" I asked.

"Your neck."

I licked my lips, a little startled, a little afraid. A whole lot confused.

"What do you mean?"

"I mean to bite you, Ivy Birkeland of Earth. I mean to fuck you at the same time. Claim you. It won't be gentle. It can't be, not with my fangs piercing your flesh for the first time. Not with the mating fist locking us together. We'll be fucking for hours."

I whimpered at the thought of *hours*.

I tugged at his hold, and he released me. I flew off the bed, went across the room to put as much distance between us as possible, which wasn't all that much. This wasn't the Ritz.

"Don't mess with me, Zenos."

"I'm not."

"You didn't get what you wanted, so you're here like a petulant child."

"I'm not," he repeated. "I'm angry."

"Don't you dare put that anger on me. So you're mad I left. Too bad."

"I don't put anything on you." He raised his hand to his chest. "It's all on me."

I stared. Then stared some more. Had I heard him correctly? "What?"

"It's my fault. All of it." He came over to me again. Now I was in the corner, Zenos's large body blocking me in. His hands settled on the wall by my head. There was no escape. I could physically move him, we both knew that, but I wanted to know what he meant, what he would do. Why he was here.

"Ivy... I love you."

I gasped. The sound fell from my lips as my chest ached.

"Then why didn't you—"

"Because I love you."

"That doesn't make any sense."

His hands came up and cupped my cheeks. "You are everything to me. I couldn't stand the idea of you dying because of me. I love you enough not to bite you."

"Like Astra and Barek," I replied.

His thumb brushed over my cheek, and he smeared wetness. It was then I realized I was crying.

"Until last night, yes. Barek has loved Astra for decades. He's stood by her, watched out for her. Protected her even when she didn't need it. But he refused to bite her."

"I don't think they even had sex until last night," I guessed.

"Yes, I agree. Barek refused to harm her by his bite. He loved her too much."

"But they trusted the antidote. You didn't. You didn't trust me."

I kissed her then, not able to wait a moment longer. "I didn't trust *me*." I clarified when I lifted my lips.

"Oh, Zenos," I whispered. "You can't deny yourself what you've been waiting for so long."

"I haven't until you came into the bar. I had been waiting for you. I hadn't wanted to bite anyone until I kissed your lips, licked your pussy, fucked it good and hard."

I wiggled a bit at his dark words.

"It's been so hard to deny what was between us. How I felt. I was trying to be strong for both of us."

I waggled my eyebrows. "Haven't you learned I'm pretty strong myself?"

He growled then, lifted me up and tossed me onto the bed. I bounced but didn't pop up to fight. I laid there, waiting. I was right where I wanted to be.

"I love you, Zenos. I want you to bite me. To claim me. Make me yours. Completely."

He licked his lips, took in every inch of me. I waited one heartbeat, then another. Then he pounced.

"Mine," he breathed as he worked my shirt up and off my body, stripped me of my bra and panties.

He stood at the foot of the bed, shucked every bit of his clothes until he was bare as well. His cock with thick and hard, pointed right at me. I couldn't see any sign of the mating fist he'd spoken of, and my pussy clenched knowing how tight a fit he was normally.

How was he going to fit when he claimed me?

I licked my lips, eager for him.

"Do that again and my cock will be in that mouth, mate, not that pussy."

I shook my head, curled my finger to beckon him to me. "Another time. Claim me."

"As you command," he said and crawled over me. Kissed me. Everywhere. My lips, my jaw, my neck, my breasts. Down one leg and then back up the other. He even kissed my clit.

"Zenos," I said.

"Mate," he replied, settling on top of me, nudging my thighs apart. His cock slid over my thigh, pre-cum smearing into a wet streak.

"Mate," I repeated.

He slid into me in one long, slow stroke and I gasped. He

groaned. My back arched, my hands went to his waist. He fucked me then, slow and steady, his lips on mine.

He swallowed my moans of pleasure until he finally lifted his head, looked me in the eye.

"It's time."

I nodded and angled my head. Offered myself. All of me.

"I love you," I told him, giving him the only words that were necessary.

"I love you," he replied, lowering his head to my neck. He didn't wait, didn't delay one second longer, piercing my skin with those sharp fangs.

The pain was searing but fleeting, replaced by an orgasm so fierce I almost blacked out. I felt him swell inside me. Stretch me. Thicken. I tried to move, but between his bite and the mating fist that now locked us together, I couldn't go anywhere.

Zenos groaned against my neck, I felt the vibrations of it as our chests were pressed together. He came, filling me hotly with his seed, but he didn't get smaller, didn't pull out.

He couldn't.

His fangs slipped from me, his tongue licking over the twin wounds at the base of my neck.

"Mine," he growled and began to fuck me, as much as he could with us being locked together.

I cupped his ass, pulled him into me. The pleasure had never receded. I was on the brink of a second orgasm, which I knew would be as intense as the first.

I couldn't stop it. I let go, gave in to what it was to be his.

"Ivy. You are mine," he said as he came again and I followed.

"Mine!" I cried, lost in the pleasure.

This was what it was like being mates. Perfect. Whole. One with another.

I realized in that instant that Rogue 5 wasn't my home. Astra Legion wasn't my home. It was Zenos.

He was my home.

———

Ready for more? Read Her Cyborg Warriors next!

Professional surfer Mikki Tanaka did not want to leave her beloved Hawaii, her ocean waves, or the vibrant sea life she works so hard to protect. But the police don't approve of her protests and aggressive tactics—and she lands in jail. Her choice? Ten years, or life as an Interstellar Bride. Never one to shy away from adventure, she decides to take her chances in the stars—with not one, but two sexy as hell alpha warriors on The Colony.

Surnen, a Prillon Warrior and trusted doctor, has been waiting for a bride for years. Banished to The Colony, he's given up all hope, until a black-haired beauty instantly steals his heart and his breath. But the highly disciplined doctor likes protocols and control, in bed and out of it. His second agrees. Unfortunately, his new bride has a wild streak, a thirst for danger, and an appetite for violence that both shocks and thrills him. When her penchant for stirring up trouble brings danger to The Colony, he'll stop at nothing to save her.

Nothing at all.

Click here to get Her Cyborg Warriors now!

A SPECIAL THANK YOU TO MY READERS...

Want more? I've got **hidden** bonus content on my web site *exclusively* for those on my mailing list.

If you are already on my email list, you don't need to do a thing! Simply scroll to the bottom of my newsletter emails and click on the *super-secret* link.

Not a member? What are you waiting for? In addition to ALL of my bonus content (great new stuff will be added regularly) you will be the first to hear about my newest release the second it hits the stores—AND you will get a free book as a special welcome gift.

Sign up now! http://freescifiromance.com

FIND YOUR INTERSTELLAR MATCH!

YOUR mate is out there. Take the test today and discover your perfect match. Are you ready for a sexy alien mate (or two)?

VOLUNTEER NOW!

interstellarbridesprogram.com

DO YOU LOVE AUDIOBOOKS?

Grace Goodwin's books are now available as
audiobooks...everywhere.

LET'S TALK SPOILER ROOM!

Interested in joining my **Sci-Fi Squad**? Meet new like-minded sci-fi romance fanatics and chat with Grace! Get excerpts, cover reveals and sneak peeks before anyone else. Be part of a private Facebook group that shares pictures and fun news! Join here:

https://www.facebook.com/groups/scifisquad/

***

Want to talk about Grace Goodwin books with others? Join the **SPOILER ROOM** and spoil away! Your GG BFFs are waiting! (And so is Grace)

Join here:

https://www.facebook.com/groups/ggspoilerroom/

GET A FREE BOOK!

Join my mailing list to be the first to know of new releases, free books, special prices and other author giveaways.

http://freescifiromance.com

ALSO BY GRACE GOODWIN

Cyborg Seduction

Her Cyborg Beast

Cyborg Fever

Rogue Cyborg

Cyborg's Secret Baby

Her Cyborg Warriors

Interstellar Brides® Program: The Virgins

The Alien's Mate

His Virgin Mate

Claiming His Virgin

His Virgin Bride

His Virgin Princess

Interstellar Brides® Program: Ascension Saga

Ascension Saga, book 1

Ascension Saga, book 2

Ascension Saga, book 3

Trinity: Ascension Saga - Volume 1

Ascension Saga, book 4

Ascension Saga, book 5

Ascension Saga, book 6

Faith: Ascension Saga - Volume 2

Ascension Saga, book 7

Ascension Saga, book 8

Ascension Saga, book 9

Destiny: Ascension Saga - Volume 3

ABOUT GRACE

Grace Goodwin is a USA Today and international bestselling author of Sci-Fi and Paranormal romance with nearly one million books sold. Grace's titles are available worldwide in multiple languages in ebook, print and audio formats. Two best friends, one left-brained, the other right-brained, make up the award-winning writing duo that is Grace Goodwin. They are both mothers, escape room enthusiasts, avid readers and intrepid defenders of their preferred beverages. (There may or may not be an ongoing tea vs. coffee war occurring during their daily communications.) Grace loves to hear from readers.

All of Grace's books can be read as sexy, stand-alone adventures. But be careful, she likes her heroes hot and her love scenes hotter. You have been warned...

www.gracegoodwin.com
gracegoodwinauthor@gmail.com

CPSIA information can be obtained
at www.ICGtesting.com
Printed in the USA
BVHW041004120121
597542BV00027B/1822